MISFIT LIL CHEATS THE HANGROPE

Misfit Lil was riding for a fall. She'd chosen to intervene in the fortunes of a wagon train of emigrants, incompetently led by erstwhile outlaw, Luke Reiner, their guide. Lil's first mistake was to save a bunch of children when the wagons were caught in a blizzard, then to enlist Jackson Farraday's assistance. This only resulted in a bloody fight with Reiner. Lil's interventions have serious consequences when Jackson is accused of murder. Can she save him from hanging?

CHAP O'KEEFE

MISFIT LIL CHEATS THE HANGROPE

Complete and Unabridged

LINFORD
Leicester

First published in Great Britain in 2009

First Linford Edition
published 2011

The moral right of the author has been asserted

British Library CIP Data

O'Keefe, Chap.
  Misfit Lil cheats the hangrope. - -
(Linford western library)
  1. Western stories.
  2. Large type books.
  I. Title II. Series
  823.9′14–dc22

  ISBN 978–1–44480–591–8

Published by
F. A. Thorpe (Publishing)
Anstey, Leicestershire

Set by Words & Graphics Ltd.
Anstey, Leicestershire
Printed and bound in Great Britain by
T. J. International Ltd., Padstow, Cornwall

This book is printed on acid-free paper

1

Stray Wagon Train

Miss Lilian Goodnight was reputed to be hard to shock. Indeed, it was she who was apt to shock the country around Silver Vein; what some considered her outrageous behaviour had earned her the moniker Misfit Lil.

But the wagon train came as a shock to Lil.

And it kept right on producing shocks of one sort or another to which she wasn't immune for several tense and troubling weeks in the early spring.

Lil sighted the wagon train from a vantage point high on a lonely, windswept ridge in the northernmost section of her father's Flying G range where she had spent the bleakest part of winter manning an isolated line camp.

The word manning could be used advisedly because, notwithstanding youth and gender, Lil knew as much about range work and the rugged country — part of a land she loved — as any of her pa's forty-and-found cowpunchers.

The wagon train was out of place and out of time, strung haphazardly like two rows of child's pull-along toys across the speckled greys, ochres and dark greens of a sparsely grown granitic landscape still obscured in places by unmelted snow.

It was out of place because most of the emigrants bound for California and other points on the Far West frontier traversed Utah in the vicinity of the Great Salt Lake, many miles to the north of this difficult stretch. For reasons unreadable to Lil, the small train had looped south.

It was out of time because the movement of hopeful settlers by wagon train had about come to an end. Also, more immediately than representing the tail end of a passing era, the cavalcade

Lil saw was daringly early in the season for travel through mountainous ranges where snow fell from mid-October and sometimes remained on the ground right up until July.

To Lil's experienced gaze, the weather today was due to turn treacherous. A glint in her grey eyes generally denoted she had some playful mischief afoot. Now, it was a glint of concern.

A bank of huge black clouds had piled up on the jagged horizon. That was ominous. A snowstorm was in the offing. Lil knew swirling blasts of the icy white stuff could reduce the wagon drivers' visibility nigh to zero, rip at the big rigs' canvas covers and penetrate maybe greenhorn travellers' store-bought Eastern clothing like knife thrusts. The wagons' progress would become blind and perilous.

The breeze stiffened, blowing from the north.

In automatic reflex, Lil's trusty grey cow-pony Rebel turned his rump to the rising wind, tail whipping between his legs. But she had trained her mount from a foal and he responded obediently when she pulled his head round again and set them off downslope for the wagons.

Men were moving up and down the length of the train yelling orders, checking harness and gear and putting ropes on the farm animals that walked in the space between the two lines of wagons. Lil let her eyes rove over the emigrants.

One of the party sat on horseback off to one side. He was a burly man she took to be the emigrants' hired trail guide. He was dressed like a frontiersman in buckskins similar to those favoured by herself and her friend and reluctant idol, the civilian Army scout Jackson Farraday. But buckskins looked right when she saw them on Jackson and she felt comfortable in hers. This blocky, bulky man with a fleshy but hard face was neither right nor comfortable in his duds.

He saw her coming and tensed — till

he saw she was a girl and therefore, he possibly thought, of no account.

'Who you staring at, gal? What do you want?' he called, his face darkening.

'Not staring,' Lil said calmly. 'Just wondering what y'all plan on doing.'

'Is that so?' the guide snarled. 'Well, damned if that'd be any business o' your'n, missy. Hightail it!'

'Don't get proddy, mister. I figured I could give you strangers some help is all. Humdinger of a storm a-coming . . . a blizzard, I'd opine.'

'Damn me — ain't that the truth, gal!' the guide said sarcastically. 'We got eyes of our own.'

'Are you the wagonmaster?' Lil asked.

'I speak for him! I'm his scout and guide. Winton Petrie's the captain. He gathered these farming folks together back in Missouri and they signed up with the wagon train.'

Lil could imagine how it was. No single wagon stood much of a chance of completing a lone trek across dangerous, unknown country — across

5

deserts, over mountains, through Indian territory. It was still not much more than half a lifetime since such perilous, lengthy journeys had been for none but missionaries and mountain men. In a group, it would still be tough on the men, and tougher again on their womenfolk and children. But they could travel together sharing challenges and troubles; sharing hopes for starting over in fresh country, like California or Oregon, that held the promise of a bright future.

'What is it, Reiner?' another voice boomed.

Lil's eyes went to the speaker. He was in his early fifties, a rugged man with the hard-worn looks of a farmer, stepping out alongside the lead wagon, which was drawn by oxen. An imposingly heavy beard and moustache, as well as his carrying voice, lent him an air of authority.

Reiner was dismissive.

'Some damnfool gal, Cap'n Petrie. Spouting off 'bout a blizzard, as if I hadn't steered the train a far piece already across Kansas and Colorado.'

'You don't know the wind that blows off our mountains,' Lil warned. 'Haven't you heard what that range is called? Wasatch.'

'Wasatch so what!'

Lil let her eyes roll.

'You're the damn fool, Mister Reiner.'

Petrie said, 'How's that, missy?'

'Wasatch is the Ute words Wuhu' Seai spoken in American English,' Lil said, striving to be patient. 'My friend Jackson Farraday told me that.'

'Jackson Farraday?'

Lil became proud. 'Mister Farraday is a real scout who works for the Army. He's reliably versed in the lore of this land . . . more like the old trailblazers than your Mister Reiner, I'd say.'

Reiner let out a roar of anger at Lil's slighting implication.

'Git, you sassy brat, before you feel the cut of a whip!'

But Winton Petrie stayed him. 'Hold on, Reiner, the kid ain't told all yet, has she? What's so all-fired bothersome in this Wasatch word?'

Lil drew herself up in her saddle and said, as primly and straight-faced as she could, 'Wuhu' Seai means a frozen — *thing*.'

'How interesting!' a fresh voice put in. 'What sort of thing?'

At the front of the covered wagon behind Petrie, a girl had appeared. She had light brown hair done in two pigtails beneath a frilly bonnet, dimples and a smattering of freckles across a pretty nose.

'Now then, Honesty!' Petrie said. 'Be a good daughter and speak when you're spoken to.' But his tone was indulgent.

'Why, hullo, friend!' Lil said. 'Pleased to meet you. I'm Lil Goodnight.' And she proceeded to answer the girl's question, taking a liking to her promising quickness and eagerness for knowledge.

Once upon an infamous time, a similar approach had led Lil into all kinds of trouble when her pa, Ben Goodnight, had memorably sent her to a finishing school in Boston where she'd educated her fellow pupils, mostly the over-protected daughters of Eastern gentlefolk, in the ways of nature and the world. The extra-curricular favour had led to her expulsion.

'It's like this,' Lil explained to the girl in the wagon. 'A thing is what's also called a man's cock, or his pecker, or his tool — or a half-hundred other names. You see, a Ute chief informed Jackson that many Indians used to live between Heber and Provo. One day at the dawn of their history, the braves were out hunting when a mighty blizzard sprang up and they lost a man. When they found him he was dead and his thing was frozen stiff. So, because Indians weren't silly about this stuff before the Europeans changed them, and maybe as a warning, they named the mountains for his misfortune.'

Honesty Petrie giggled excitedly. 'Oh, did you hear that, Luke?' she said to Reiner. 'What a terrible, wasteful tragedy!' For a moment, she was flirtatiously arch beyond her innocent years, which looked no more than seventeen in sum. Then, more demurely to Lil, 'I can't wait to tell your interesting story to my friend Prudence!'

But Reiner was seething and her father had gone red in the face.

'No, you shall not, young lady!' Petrie said. 'Prudence's father is a parson. You forget yourself. The Reverend Hannigan leads this party spiritually and he don't abide dirty talk.'

Reiner produced a sickeningly false smile for Honesty.

'Your pa is right, honey,' he said ingratiatingly. 'A nice lady like yourself shouldn't be listening to coarse windies.'

Chided, Honesty dropped her face and sighed daintily, but from beneath the frill of her bonnet she flashed Lil a look that was surely rebellious if not conspiratorial.

Though Lil was irritated to hear her information dismissed as a coarse tale, it wasn't an apt time for palaver. The wind was starting to whistle and bend and pluck at the sparse tussocks of grass.

'Well, anyway,' Lil said, addressing the men, 'less'n you gents fancy being found dead with your important parts in a state of irregular stiffness, now's the time to turn your wagons and livestock off this exposed trail and head for shelter.'

'And where do we find this shelter?' Petrie asked.

'Follow me. The Flying G — that's my father's outfit — has a line camp in a valley only a mile east. Your wagons can be there in a half-hour. In the lee of the valley's northern flank and its timber, you'll have a mite of protection, and there's watering places and patches of willows along the creek.'

'I see,' Petrie said, starting to give the proposal consideration.

'I gathered the best part of my pa's herd in this section and drove them to the valley for the winter. The cabin was warm and snug for me with plenty of firewood handy, food stores and books. Only hard work I had to do was chop holes in the ice on the creek so the cows could keep drinking.'

Quick, frowning reflection made her realize that wasn't the entire truth of it. 'Oh, and kill a mountain lion that was stalking a calf, and chase off a pack of wolves, and haul a big old steer out of a tangle of brush.'

Reiner scoffed disbelievingly. 'The kid's full of bullshit, Cap'n! 'Sides, her pa won't want our critters mixing in with his longhorns. Either that or his waddies'll steal 'em.'

Lil's eyes flashed. 'That's a lie! The Flying G aren't thieves! We can fix a rope corral for your domestic stuff easy.'

The wagoners' guide rudely turned his back on her.

'Keep 'em rolling!' Reiner yelled, the wind seeming to snatch and spread the word as it left his coarse lips. 'There's a pass up ahead. We can get offa this damn mountain before the storm hits if we hurry.'

'Sure, Luke!' a wagoner called back. 'Time's a-wastin'!'

Lil knew the truth of it was that the pass Luke Reiner saw as an escape route was anything but. Most storm winds were funnelled through it with added velocity. The wagon train and its occupants would be lashed there ferociously by the coming sleet or snow.

Lil felt foreboding as a hard knot within her stomach. These foolish men, especially their guide, Luke Reiner, wouldn't take her advice. Plainly, the arrogant Reiner would soon as give an arm as give anyone else a say in directing the wagon train. That plus, she suspected, he liked to keep the wagonmaster's pretty daughter impressed . . .

She was sorry for the wagoners' womenfolk and the buttons who had no choice but to accompany their elders on the long and gruelling adventure. But she could do no more. If only Jackson were here! He would know what to do for the best. He always knew!

It was some months since she'd last seen her reluctant hero, but during her sojourn at the line camp, he'd never been far from her thoughts. Not for long could she thrust remembrance of his solid reliability out of her mind.

Flakes of snow began to fall, whirling and dancing on the wind in wild pirouettes at first. The wagon women who were afoot clutched their skirts to stop the wind from lifting them, and ran at their men's urging to climb into the wagons.

A wagon train — lumbering, heavily laden — generally moved at a speed of around two miles an hour. Able-bodied women and children customarily walked beside the wagons, like the men. Emigrant parties averaged ten miles a day. With good weather, the 2,000 mile journey from Missouri to California or Oregon would take about five months.

With a maximum load of passengers, Reiner was now attempting to force four or five miles an hour out of these wagons. Lil knew the draught animals, oxen or horses, would not be able to sustain such a pace. It was unlikely Petrie's expedition would even make the pass without capsizes or other accidents.

The snow was changing swiftly with each gust of wind from feathery lightness to sharp, stabbing needle-points. Hurled on by the rushing wind, it laid quickly. In an incredibly short time, the slope before Lil was covered by a thickening white carpet.

The wagon train vanished before her narrowed, watering eyes into a relent-less, blinding snow storm.

What to do?

She tugged down her hat-brim, tied it securely under her chin, turned her collar up around her neck till it shielded her cold ears, and pulled up a neckerchief to protect her face from the stinging lash of icy snow. Winter was coming back with a vengeance, taking what had to be a late, unfortunate, last fling.

It was going to be a first-class

blizzard for sure. Landmarks were rapidly disappearing in the whiteout conditions, though she had every confidence Rebel would know their trail back to the line camp and she had few worries for her own safety.

Her thoughts were with the women and children of the wagon train — especially the pretty one called Honesty Petrie. She had a weird feeling she'd met her before though she knew she couldn't have.

Yet it was overlaid by the other feeling she had, that if she didn't do something she might never see Honesty or her companions again.

How could a spurned country girl and her horse help?

Preoccupied, Lil gave Rebel's neck a gentle pat. 'This looks like it's going to get bad,' she murmured. 'Better turn back to the cabin for now.'

2

Victims of the Blizzard

The single-roomed cabin was more of a shack, unpainted, ramshackle and nestled by a fork of the still partly frozen creek. But it was sound and snug with a solid cast-iron stove and a leak-free tin chimney. The bunk was comfortable, the plain deal kitchen table was solid and the chairs were firm enough for a girl of Lil's modest weight, though they creaked some in the joints. Best, it had a shelf of books, ranging from classics to dime novels, which had helped Lil while away the winter days when she'd been snowed in.

On entering after she'd quartered Rebel in the attached lean-to stable, Lil went to the shelf, thinking it might offer the means to distract her troubled thoughts from the possible plight into which Luke Reiner was leading his hapless charges.

She thought, too, it might be a good moment to crack the seal on the last bottle of her stock of imported whiskey. Lil, the daughter of a prosperous cattleman, had developed tastes for the best in everything at a young age. This was no cheap redeye. Gilt lettering on the black label said, 'Very Old Scotch Whisky.'

After a cold ride, it would warm the heart, no question.

At the last moment, she paused. Maybe she should save the fine liquor; an odd premonition told her she might need to have her wits about her before the blizzard was past. Wouldn't do to get drunk, or even a mite giddy.

Reading that would warm the heart might be better advised.

Putting aside the whiskey, she turned back to the bookshelf. Her eyes had barely scanned a title or two before they fell on *A Christmas Carol*. And suddenly it fell into place.

She knew at last of whom she was reminded by the pretty girl with the wagon train — not a real person at all, but a character in that dilapidated book illustrated by hand-coloured engravings and more than thirty years old.

Honesty Petrie was Scrooge's niece come to life!

She took down the well-worn book and flipped through the pages till she found it:

She was very pretty; exceedingly so. With a dimpled, surprised-looking, capital face; a ripe little mouth, that seemed made to be kissed — as no doubt it was; all kinds of good little dots about her chin, that melted into one another when she laughed; and the sunniest pair of eyes you ever saw in any little creature's head. Altogether she was what you would have called provoking, you know; but satisfactory, too. Oh, perfectly satisfactory!

Almost like this Chuck Dickens feller had met her, Lil commented to herself. This had to be a very odd coincidence, but it also hit her harder than ever that Honesty and her companions might not survive the storm or the inevitable accidents as the wagon train toiled blindly into the extreme conditions of the mountain pass on which Reiner had set his sights.

Reading the passage in the book convinced Lil she was meant to do something about the wagon train and its innocent greenhorns. Reiner probably had, and would, face many grim struggles in guiding the Petrie party to their Promised Land. He'd argue this was his responsibility and included how he got the job done. But some folk naturally depended on people. You couldn't let them down. In Lil's estimation a girl had a full share of responsibilities no less than a man, in this or any other country.

She couldn't put them aside because a man had bullied her into accepting she should. She'd have to go out again.

She took down a stiff canvas windbreaker from a wooden peg and shrugged into it. She thrust her hands into leather mittens. Given the worsening conditions, experience told her she'd make as better time to the pass on foot than on horseback. In the blinding snow, she would likely have to dismount and lead her reliable Rebel much of the way, sure-footed and knowledgeable though the cow-pony might be. On a hunch, she took from the lean-to a coiled horsehair lariat which she slipped over her right shoulder.

The snow crunched under her boots as she went out into the storm. In places, the stuff had already drifted, making her stride awkward and slowing her progress, but she went forth, determined, and came to the top of the first ridge.

Out of the shelter of the valley, the late-season blizzard had turned into a howling gale. The tops of the pines were bending and tossing in the wind, shaking off what little snow settled on them.

It took her a long half-hour to struggle up to the pass. There a scene of chaos awaited her, revealed to sore, red-rimmed eyes in glimpses through the icy white blasts.

The lumbering wagons had come to grief at the head of the pass. A heavily laden Conestoga had capsized. It could have been driven off the trail's edge into a snow-filled gully and toppled, or it could have been simply blown over. The wind was fierce enough. Whatever, it had blocked the narrow passage for the rest of the train. The wagons were neither able to go around it or turn back. Now they were at the mercy of the cruel elements. At a standstill, they rocked and swayed and the wind ripped at the canvas coverings.

The men — and the women, too — ran to and fro, trying to secure spooked livestock and tie down their precious, exposed possessions. The gale was intensified by the narrow chink the pass provided. In its teeth, it was hard work for the wagoners just to keep their footing.

To one side, a group of the youngest children had been gathered in a huddle, supervised by two older girls. One Lil recognized by her pigtails as Honesty Petrie; the other she assumed might be Honesty's friend Prudence, daughter of the party's sky-pilot. Their position was desperate. If the storm persisted any length of time, and without movement to stimulate their circulation, they would be frozen.

Lil decided she'd take it upon herself to shepherd the pathetic group to the warmth and shelter of the Flying G line cabin.

'Hey, Honesty!' she cried, but the words were whipped away and lost in the tumult of the blizzard. She had to move in much closer before she could repeat her holler and be heard.

Honesty jumped. 'Oh, Prudence — look it's the wild girl I told you about! The one who wanted to lead us to the safety of her valley. She must have come to help us.'

Prudence was a strapping, well-built girl of similar age to Honesty. Less robust wagon women were struggling to help their menfolk save the buffeted wagons and stock, but clearly she had been assigned the task of assisting the daintier daughter of the wagonmaster to look after the children. Though her face might be just frozen into stiffness, to Lil her expression had a sullen cast.

Prudence didn't seem to understand or share her companion's pleasure at the appearance of this female who'd loomed up startlingly out of the driving snow in a man's long coat and pants.

'You told me Mister Reiner saw her off,' she said bluntly. 'Maybe she's come to gloat at us in our predicament.'

'No!' Lil shouted above the shriek of the wind. 'It's like Honesty says — I want to lend a hand.'

'Oh, Lil, how kind you are!' Honesty said. Then, with less spirit, 'Lil — what should we do? I fear these buttons will freeze to death!'

Lil privately agreed. Many already looked sickly youngsters and none was properly outfitted for long exposure to such weather.

'Get them to stamp their feet and slap their arms about their bodies,' she said. 'Show them how. Get them to rub soft snow over their faces, specially their noses and ears. It'll protect them.'

'Since you live hereabouts, tell us,' Prudence said tonelessly. 'How long will this foul weather rage?'

'Maybe hours, maybe all day and all night. I'll tell you what — we need to get these kids out of it for sure.'

Honesty's brow puckered. 'But Mister Reiner said it would be dangerous for them to wander off. That's why Prudence and I are in charge.'

Suddenly, as though mention of his name had conjured him up, Luke Reiner joined them. His slate-coloured eyes were cold and, being set close together, gave his hard features a look of piggish cunning.

'You again, whatever you called yourself!' he said to Lil. 'I told you to scat, didn't I? Well, do it! But first I'll take that rope offa you. We'll use it to tie stuff down.'

He reached for the coiled lariat, but Lil stepped back, a gleam in her eye and a revolver in her hand. The last came out of nowhere from inside the folds of her canvas windbreaker.

'No, you won't! I've got other notions for it.'

'Jesus!' Reiner said. 'You're just too damned salty, gal. You wait — see you again and I'll remember this!'

One of the wagoners was calling him and he stumped away hurriedly — without the rope.

'Bravo, Lil!' Honesty said, clapping her hands together. 'Luke can be high-handed from time to time. You told him off properly.'

Prudence asked ungraciously, 'Wasn't that pushing it too far? I've no time for Reiner and can't see what Honesty sees in him, ever. Why do you need the rope?'

'To save the littl'uns,' Lil said. 'Here, they're trapped, but tie us all together with the rope I can lead you and your charges to the safety of my shack. It ain't a big place, but there's room and grub enough for everyone — and a grand stove with heaps of firewood.'

The wagon train girls caught on immediately to Lil's plan. Roped together, no one would slip and fall unnoticed by the others; no one afflicted by snow-blindness would wander from the trail and become buried in some awful drift, not to be found until a thaw came.

Not bothering to check with their busy elders, Honesty and Prudence helped Lil put the scheme into immediate action. The circumstances didn't allow for much talk. They had to concentrate on tying the right sort of knots with fingers numb and clumsy from the cold. It was no time for argument. But Lil could have reassured the girls from the East that she'd experienced such storms before in her life, and her way was the best way.

The blizzard was occasioned by the collision of an immense Arctic cold front with warm, moisture-laden air from the Gulf of Mexico. Within a few hours, the advancing cold front had caused a temperature drop from the relatively balmy to ten degrees Fahrenheit below freezing. Such a fast-moving wave of cold was accompanied by high winds and heavy snow.

What made the storm potentially deadly to the stray wagon train was its timing, its suddenness, the spell of settled spring weather that had preceded it, and the inexperience of the wagonmaster and his so-called guide.

The strong wind and the powdery consistency of the snow reduced visibility to zero. In less than two hours, snow had settled to a depth of six inches and more. Without Lil's familiarity with the land — she knew it like the proverbial back of her hand — Honesty, Prudence and the wagons' children would have become totally disorientated and lost within minutes.

But they came with no dire mishap to the Flying G line shack. Lil hustled them into its cosiness and firmly shut the door on the whistling nor'wester.

A dozen small faces that had been frozen and stiff with cold were soon wreathed in smiles.

Naturally, Honesty and Prudence, being older, were more aware of the disaster that had befallen their parents. They were deeply worried about what would become of families and possessions they'd left behind under assault in the bleak, barren, wind- and snow-swept pass.

Honesty bit a wind-cracked lip. 'Is there nothing we could have done? Father spent a thousand dollars to outfit for this journey. Our wagon alone cost four hundred. We had oxen to pull it because they cost thirty dollars a head. Mules or horses were seventy-five, bottom.'

Lil shook her head. 'At the end of the

storm, be it later today or tomorrow, Mister Petrie and his followers will be thankful for their lives!'

She didn't need Honesty to tell her the overland journey from the Mid-West to Oregon and California was an expensive undertaking, being six months of travel across two thousand miles of difficult country.

Winton Petrie would have had other reasons for choosing oxen. As a farmer, he'd know they were stronger and easier to work than horses or mules. They were also less likely to be stolen by Indians and would be handy as farm animals when he reached his destination. Oxen could survive on sparse graze and were less likely to stray from camp. The main argument against them was they were apt to be cantankerous when hot and thirsty and were known to cause stampedes in a rush to reach water.

Lil didn't think oxen would take too kindly to a blizzard either.

Prudence's thoughts turned to the

stores and furniture that would be spoiled.

'I know one family of four has eight hundred pounds of flour, two hundred pounds of lard, seven hundred pounds of bacon, two hundred pounds of beans, one hundred pounds of fruit, seventy-five pounds of coffee and twenty-five pounds of salt. I'm sure others have similar. Then there are all the tables and chairs, and beds and chests . . . To think of all that being lost!'

'Tough,' Lil said, surprised at a preacher's daughter's meticulous recording of a family's material wealth. She added reassuringly, 'But those ol' Conestogas and the like can carry a load of two thousand five hundred pounds, though I figure three-fourths of that would be safer.'

She didn't like to agree that once the gale had ripped the linseed-oiled, waterproof tops off the hoop-shaped ribs of the wagons, all the emigrants' treasure could be ruined or blown away.

And it was mostly down to one man's

bull-headed stupidity.

Luke Reiner . . .

What was he thinking of, setting himself up as the party's scout and guide? It was criminal. And why had he brought them so far south?

Lil began to wonder about his credentials and figured he must have some other, secret motive.

She said to the wagon girls, 'I'm going to talk about this to my friend Jackson Farraday. He works for the Army as a civilian scout and is the most experienced man on the frontier. Your pa should hire him straight away. He'd sort out this mess, I know.'

Honesty sighed. 'I hope someone can, but at the moment I can't help fearing the worst.'

'Cheer up,' Lil said. 'When the storm abates, I'll point your wagons to the nearest town, which is Silver Vein. Your folks can get the broken things fixed up there, and meet with Jackson. They'll all like him, I know.'

In fact, it wasn't going to be that easy.

3

Fighting Talk

Four days later, in the cold of the early morning, Jackson Farraday rode out to the meadow just north of Silver Vein where Winton Petrie's expedition had camped after the unfortunate experience in the mountain pass. Several of the battered wagons had had to be abandoned and most of the rigs left were in a sorry state. The emigrants' gaunted livestock, penned in makeshift corrals, looked no better.

As it turned out, Jackson went not at the bidding of young Lil Goodnight but at the suggestion of the gruff but fair commanding officer of Fort Dennis, Colonel Brook Lexborough.

'The emigrants approached us for help and we gave what was allowed within the limits of department policy on civil matters,' Lexborough said. 'Their leader, Mister Winton Petrie, and their pastor, the Reverend James Hannigan, told me they'd heard about your qualifications from Miss Goodnight. She'd sung your praises highly.'

Jackson sighed. Much as he liked Lil, her adulation could be embarrassingly wearying for a man twice her age and often gave rise to tension between them, especially on the past occasions when circumstances (or occasionally, he'd suspected, Lil's contrivance) had thrown them together, alone.

Age disparity was not seen as an obstacle to partnerings in the West. The ratio of men to women in some territories was very unbalanced, sometimes as much as eight to one. Men competed for whatever female attractions hadn't been spoiled by drudgery and sometimes harsh living. Vulnerable girls saw older men as more stable. But Jackson was personally cautious in the matter. He didn't want to be set up for a future in which he might wake up a decrepit old man bedded with a wife still in her prime.

Friendship was possible; romance he forbade himself, a hazard for which his accomplishments as a true frontiersman left him unpractised.

But of this, which tossed about his feelings like leaves in a storm, he said nothing to Colonel Lexborough.

'I hear Lil Goodnight was the heroine of the hour. The gossip in town has it she saved the wagon children from the horrors of the blizzard.'

Lexborough confirmed Lil's latest claim to local fame and Jackson felt absurdly pleased that the exploit wasn't one that could be used to boost her notoriety. Miss Purity Wadsworth, sin-hunting president of the Silver Vein Ladies' Temperance Society, and the Reverend Titus Fisher, sniffy sky-pilot of the parish, would surely be disappointed.

Now, reaching the emigrants' camp, which was coming alive after the night, Jackson asked a small child watching two men already working on fixing a busted wheel where he could find Mister Petrie. He wondered if the skinny kid who gave directions in a piping voice was one of those rescued by Lil, but he didn't ask.

Petrie was finishing breakfast. A second man was seated with him by a dying cookfire, his eyes fixed on the embers but his contemplation probably elsewhere. A girl with pigtails, neither child nor woman, was collecting up dirty dishes in a tin bowl.

The bearded wagonmaster got up with an outstretched hand. A palm met Jackson's. Eyes surrounded by the crinkles of worry-lines stared into his.

'Mister Farraday, I figure. Much obliged you've ridden over. This here is the Reverend Hannigan, who — uh — leads us in matters of faith and advises us in our duties to the Almighty.'

'Admirable, I'm sure,' Jackson said politely.

James Hannigan was stern-faced. Dressed austerely in black, he nodded and grunted. He was a tall, thin man with piercing, hard eyes and a rat-trap of a mouth. He could have been auditioning for the role of a Puritan forefather in turn aspiring to be an Old Testament patriarch.

The girl treated Jackson to a quick, bold smile before she left, turning away with the dishes and a saucy swing of her pigtails. Her confidence before a male stranger surprised him. Her cute, freckled nose, bright, not quite child-eyes and ripe mouth would be a provocation to any man. Despite her air of mischief, she was winsomely sweet.

Jackson caught Hannigan's frown of disapproval.

The preliminaries dispatched, Petrie got down in a firm voice to business.

'To come to the point, we'd like to put a proposition to you, Farraday. I've been convinced by our trial in the blizzard that the train is needful of the fuller knowledge of what lies ahead of us. In short, we'd like to hire you on to partner our present scout, Luke Reiner.'

'Hmm . . . ' Jackson said. 'What does Reiner have to say about this?'

The preacher broke in. 'Reiner has said nothing. What he saw as interference by the rough Flying G cow-girl rankled. He's availing himself of town accommodation while we repair the damaged wagons.'

Jackson turned to him. He didn't bother to challenge his description of Lil as a rough cow-girl. 'And what do you have to say about him being given a partner, Reverend?'

'I've no opinion, sir. Trails are my concern only in as much as I have a God-blessed duty is to keep these folks on the paths of righteousness; away from sin.'

Having solemnly sketched the parameters of his responsibility, Hannigan retreated once more into contemplation of the fire's glowing remnants, a remote expression coming over his face. Plainly, being a preacher didn't make him a conversationalist.

Jackson returned his attention to Winton Petrie.

'I'll consider your invitation for reasons I'll put bluntly. Colonel Lexborough at Fort Dennis doesn't want the blood of your women and children on his hands, which are tied by all kinds of Washington red tape. For a start, the renegade Indian Angry-he-shakes-fist is on the loose in this section with a band of young hotheads, and I respect the colonel's judgement. Aside from that consideration, the natural difficulties a wagon train will encounter on this southerly route are apt to have been underestimated by anyone who doesn't know the country.'

Petrie became defensive, taking off his hat and running his fingers through the hair on his head which had seemingly thinned as his facial hair had flourished.

'Reiner has told me he has been over the trail before, and he has a respectful affection for my daughter, Honesty.'

'Oh,' Jackson said, recalling the pigtailed young minx. 'So Reiner was appointed your trail guide for — er — undivulged reasons.'

'Not at all!' Petrie snapped. 'Honesty has found his attentions flattering is all. Howsomever, the man has given me no grounds to distrust him in any particular. He has expectations of money that will allow him to set up in a grand style in California. A widower in advancing years wants only the best for a daughter. Reiner's no boy but a grown man who might afford her the — uh — protection she needs.'

And a firm hand to keep her in line, Jackson added silently, sensing the unspoken in Petrie's harassed tone.

Meanwhile, the wagon train's situation had been checked out; overtures made.

Farraday said, 'Well, seems like I have some figuring to do, gentlemen. I'll ride back to town and palaver with your Mister Reiner. I'll let you have my decision soon.'

As he left, Honesty Petrie, who was drying the washed dishes, called out loudly, 'Good day, Mister Farraday!'

Jackson, not liking attention being drawn to him in such a fashion, merely touched his hatbrim. Sitting the saddle imposingly straight and tall, he was difficult enough to miss amid the humdrum, dirt-farmer folk of Petrie's company. Every inch a frontiersman, he plain stuck out with his long, sun-bleached hair and neat chin-beard.

Honesty chuckled flirtatiously. 'Another time, you must rest longer and let me fix you up!'

Jackson was succinct and gruff in reply.

'Miss, if I come again, it'll be to talk business with your pa. Man to man. About doing a job.'

The girl was unrepentant.

She promptly confirmed the drift of her thoughts by retorting, in lying contradiction of her given name, 'I meant fix you up with something to eat, of course!'

★ ★ ★

Luke Reiner, liquored up, was holding forth long and strong in McHendry's saloon in Silver Vein.

A half-empty whiskey bottle was on the drink-splashed mahogany bartop in front of him. In one hand he held a glass; in the other a bent, brown-paper cigarette between his thick fingers. Expression smouldered in his hard eyes as well as his words. Smoke whirled in convulsive traceries as he jabbed at the fetid air.

'This Misfit Lil gal folks here are holding up as some kinda heroine is a skinny bitch with a dirty mouth!' he told a small gathering of bemused, pre-midday drinkers who'd been discussing the blizzard rescue.

'It's me was bossing the train,' he went on. 'She had no damn right nor reason to dab a loop over their kids!'

Seeing the belligerent mood the stranger was in, no one questioned why he'd led the emigrants into their predicament in the first place.

But one of the bravest drinkers ventured, 'The buttons might well have perished in the storm contrariwise . . . '

'Bullshit! Seems to me it was all rigged. The bitch is hooked up with this Army scout Farraday who wants to get hisself a job with Winton Petrie, see? It was jest a plot to get inta the wagoners' good opinions and make me look stupid.'

'Maybe you're wronging Farraday, mister.'

'I don't think so! Petrie and his pastor pal Hannigan told me theirselves they was inviting Farraday to meet with them. They fixed it when they saw the Colonel at Fort Dennis.'

A cowboy in town to collect mail shrugged. 'So? That ain't much, is it? No call to go flyin' off'n the handle 'bout Lil anyways.'

Reiner drew himself up, bristling. An obscene oath left his lips.

'Now look here!' he flared. 'The gal was in on it all right, boy! She was trumpeting Farraday to high heaven first time we laid eyes on her. Ain't none of 'em got no right to do what they're doing behind my back. You hear me?'

'Misfit Lil is kinda salty an' a crack shot, better'n most fellers,' the cowboy said stoutly but reasonably. 'Inta pranks an' frisky, but she's a square dealer with it.'

Listening to someone else's point of view — even to reason — wasn't Reiner's strong point.

'No, she ain't! I been told she's a pest — a delinquent and the despair of her rancher father. A deluded freak in men's duds!'

The cowboy conceded, 'She's a strange 'un all right. Miss Purity Wadsworth an' her blue-nose buddies think the way she dresses an' all is a disgrace, but them's powerful strict ladies.'

'Sure it's a disgrace! The duds are a crime in point of law. And she's smitten with this ol' hobo Farraday. They're scheming to make me look small. Maybe he paid her sometime to share his blankets!'

A murmur rippled through his gathering audience. Though some of the town viewed Lilian Goodnight, daughter of respected Flying G rancher Ben Goodnight, in a bad light, it was not in an outsider like Reiner's favour to express his dislike so openly and vehemently.

Reiner took another slug of whiskey and warmed to his notions.

'Why, I ain't fooled by her duds. Fact is, underneath she's prob'ly nothing better'n a young whore! And he's a randy rascal, poking the breath outa her, doing what he pleases with ev'ry girlie part she's got!'

The gasps and sudden agitation the last accusation produced among his listeners were pleasing to Reiner. What he didn't realize was that it was occasioned by more than his juicy but slanderous diatribe.

He then became aware of a tall,

45

long-haired newcomer standing just within the batwings, silhouetted against the sunlight outside. A sixth sense told him the expression on the man's shadowed face, which he couldn't see, was thunderous.

'Mister Reiner, I guess,' the man said. 'I'm Jackson Farraday. Would you care to repeat what you just said? I mayn't've heard aright, but if I did I figure you should offer proof of your talk — which you can't — or you should bite your foul tongue pronto and apologize for the whole pack of lies!'

A dull flush reddened Reiner's heavy-fleshed face. He spat insultingly into the sawdust.

'The hell with that, sidewinder! I'll smash you to bits first.'

A deathly hush gripped the room.

Jackson said calmly, 'That's fighting talk. Step outside and I'll give you a chance to try.'

Reiner was nothing loath to accept the challenge. To put it mildly, he'd placed himself in a position where he was unable to refuse it.

'Suits me! I can whup any yeller-haired, yeller-bellied petticoat-lifter!'

No wit dared to remind him that Misfit Lil was seldom seen other than in men's pants.

4

'Too Much Man'

Jackson turned on his heel and led out of the saloon. 'We'll hear you apologize yet,' he said.

Reiner, glowering, followed him. He weaved clumsily through the tables, sending two chairs crashing.

'Me apologize?' the wagon train scout snarled. 'It's you who's gonna crawl, horny frontiersman!'

Sensitive as always about his association with young Lil Goodnight, Jackson wondered if he wasn't making some godawful mistake. Reiner's bad-mouthing of Lil had flicked his anger into life. But he had no fear about his proficiency with his fists or his ability to teach Luke Reiner a lesson.

A hubbub erupted among the witnesses in McHendry's watering-hole.

'Fight! Fight!'

The cry was taken up and spread to the main street outside. Townsfolk dropped what they were doing and began coming out from shops and workplaces to see what the fuss was about.

'Look out!' someone cried.

Jackson started to turn but was too late.

Without warning, Reiner bulled forward, closing in on him and swinging a punch at him as he reached the steps to the street. The full weight of Reiner's stocky body was behind the cowardly blow. It caught him on the side of the jaw.

Tall as he was, it lifted him physically of his feet, pitching him off the plankwalk, down the steps and into the dirt of the street.

'By Gawd!' an onlooker yelled. 'He's down an' busted already!'

But in a life that had included wilderness explorations, mining camps, logging camps, Indian fighting, railroad construction and buffalo hunting, Jackson had taken many worse tumbles. He hit the ground with a shoulder — chin down, head tucked in — and let the momentum keep him rolling till he was in a position to spring lithely to his feet.

He took a prizefighter stance and rapped, 'Put 'em up and fight fair, Reiner!'

Reiner roared and surged off the walk toward him, fists windmilling.

Jackson backed up, weaving and ducking, letting the heavier man spend his wind on his ferocity till as much of it was gone as had been knocked out of himself by his fall.

Reiner was eager and over-confident. Few of his punches contacted, but one that landed on Jackson's left biceps was numbing and made him wince. The pain flooded through his arm. He kept shifting out of range, light on his feet.

'Hit him, Farraday!' a flour-sack-aproned and impatient storekeeper said. 'We don't want no dancin' exhibition!'

Jackson got in close enough to slam two punches to Reiner's thick body. The hits were punishing but not sufficient to take significant stuffing out of him.

Breathing heavily, Reiner took the chance to trade a wicked blow before Jackson could retreat again from his reach. It was a powerful right swing that reinforced to Jackson that he really could hit and hurt, splitting the skin over his right eye. Dazed, Jackson realized he couldn't rely on wearing down Reiner before he might inflict some severe damage.

A lathered barbershop customer, still with a towel draped around him, saw the blood oozing from the cut over Jackson's eyes.

'He's bleedin', fellers!' he said eagerly. 'The wagon train hombre's gonna finish 'im!'

Bright lights swimming before his eyes, Jackson shook his head and changed tactics. He'd have to settle this faster. He stood ground and feinted with his left fist. The blocky Reiner was wide open when he drove his right into his dodging, confidently sneering face.

His knuckles smashed against teeth that seemed to shift under the impact.

Reiner, thrown back, slammed into a hitch-rail. He cussed and slid into a sitting position.

Jackson was ready for him when he pushed himself up from the ground. What he wasn't ready for was the handful of dust Reiner had craftily scooped up to fling into his face and eyes.

Momentarily blinded, Jackson stood off, holding up his fists in a guard position. His eyes streamed, but his vision was still adequate to register the sudden blur of Reiner's booted foot swinging toward his groin.

The swelling crowd was howling. Plainly, no prize-ring rules applied.

Jackson quickly turned side on, stepped forward and grabbed the man's passing ankle. Though Reiner was no mean weight, he heaved and tossed.

Reiner went over backwards, his head hitting the hard-packed road surface. His eyes glazed.

Jackson cuffed dirt and blood from his own eyes.

The watching mob had gone into a frenzy.

'Stomp him!'

'Kill him!'

'I don't fight thataway!' Jackson said, panting.

He reached down, grabbed the front of Reiner's buckskin jerkin and hauled him to his feet.

'Get up and apologize, louse! You've no grounds and no evidence to blacken Miss Goodnight.'

Groggy, swaying, Reiner said something incomprehensible but obviously derogatory. He didn't figure the fight was over and swung a senseless, looping right — his favourite punch, it seemed — at Jackson's bloodied, unamused face.

Its impact had the effect of a fistful of feathers. It also gave Jackson the right to humble him. As Reiner tottered, Jackson took his opportunity. He chopped him with a right, then a left, then another right. Each was progressively more devastating to Reiner's senses and his face.

Jackson's knuckles contacted under Reiner's square chin, crunching his teeth together and jerking his head back.

His eyes rolled. He dropped to his knees. He fell flat on his face, cradling his battered, swollen features in his arms and groaning.

When it became apparent Reiner wasn't able to get up — to fight or to apologize — Jackson said, 'I think the blowhard is through for now.'

Momentarily, Jackson towered over his huddled, unmoving body, his face taut and grim. He massaged the backs of his bruised hands, then he turned and walked away.

Behind him, he heard belly-heaving, spluttering noises as Reiner came round and threw up.

Jackson surmised that after this

Reiner would be through with Silver Vein, with insulting Lil and himself — and, more importantly, through with Petrie's wagon train.

But he was wrong.

★ ★ ★

'Roll them wagons out, boys!'

Winton Petrie's train, repaired and restocked, was on the move again, plodding away from Silver Vein in long scattered lines, a few outriders heeling their horses along the edges.

Jackson was considerably surprised that among the riders, beside himself, were both Luke Reiner and Misfit Lil.

Despite Luke Reiner's previous strong opposition to the hiring of Jackson, and being humiliatingly licked in the subsequent spectacular fight in Silver Vein, the rogue had swallowed his pride to accept the appointment of a second guide by the wagoners. His position was now held jointly with the man who'd whipped him.

He sat in his saddle rigidly, sullen and preoccupied. Jackson couldn't figure why he hadn't quit the train and said good riddance to Petrie, Hannigan and their followers, whose invitation to Jackson had cast aspersions on his competence and led to his belligerence and downfall.

But it was a long haul to California. Plenty of time for any man to find out more about what made others do the things they did; act in apparently inexplicable ways.

Jackson wondered. Could it be that after the fight Reiner had made a devilish, secret vow to his bruised, bleeding and unrepentant self to settle his, Jackson's, hash someplace on the trail?

Maybe the same thought had figured in Lil Goodnight's decision to ride along with the train, too.

'I'll help look out for you, Jackson,' she'd told him, high-spirited and confident.

'Huh? Don't you think you might be

turning into an old Mother Hen, what with nursemaiding emigrant kids and all?'

He'd hoped his joshing might make her reconsider her intention, painting the look of her interest as too domestic and tame to be acceptable for a girl of her hardy reputation. But the ploy hadn't worked.

Annoyingly, Misfit Lil was here on her favourite Rebel and with a led packhorse toting all the provisions she needed for the journey — probably more since she was outgoing and generous by nature. The rein leathers hung loose and comfortable in her hands and she rode like the born horsewoman she was.

Aside from not being an official member of the Petrie party in any capacity, Lil both didn't and did belong here.

Jackson saw it like this. All the other women, the emigrants, belonged with the wagon train but looked as though they should be at home someplace else

— either back East or already in California — cooking and sewing, keeping house, being a pleasure and comfort to their men; bearing children. Lil, however, looked as though she belonged to the land they travelled across. It was impossible to picture her bent over needlework or ironing.

But who was in and who was out of place was just damn foolish conjecture, Jackson decided, and he shoved away his studying on it.

Riding close to Lil, he called out, 'Don't you think it'd be best if you changed your mind and turned back before we get too far? This trek is going to be no fun. You don't need to drag along.'

'Try and lose me!' Lil shot back with a happy grin. 'Anywhere you are will be a damn sight more fun than moping around Silver Vein.'

Jackson didn't find her grin infectious.

'I don't know what sweet dreams are going around in your head,' he said in exasperation, 'but they're things that can't come true.'

'Oh, I don't know,' Lil said. 'I'd say there's more than a few girls here got sheep's eyes on you!'

'What does that mean?'

'Haven't you noticed? Pretty little Honesty Petrie has stopped setting her cap at Luke Reiner. She's just one who has taken to eying up the big, bold frontiersman who rubbed her old hero's nose in the dirt. Calf-love for sure, but I'll be on hand to see she knows there's another staking a prior claim!'

Jackson seethed inwardly. A second female admirer was the very last thing he wanted. For a start, it would make Lil even more determined to stick around. And his shrewd guess, based on past experience, was that her presence would be liable to lead to trouble. He shot a dagger look at Lil.

'Well, Mister Petrie's child is of no particular interest to me, and Reiner he would best've left to rot in Silver Vein. Keep clear of Reiner, you hear? Don't tell him what you've told me. You mind your business and I'll mind mine. I don't need any help.'

Lil hesitated, then nodded agreement. 'You're the boss, Jackson.'

★   ★   ★

In the closed and isolated community of the moving wagon train, it wasn't easy for Misfit Lil to keep to her agreement. Honesty Petrie and her pal, the preacher's daughter, Prudence Hannigan, cultivated her acquaintance, being fascinated by the 'wild' girl and her independent ways.

They sat on the ground the third night out from Silver Vein, a companionable trio, Lil with her back against a wheel of the Petrie wagon. The men were gathered in murmuring conversation round the fire some little way off. The womenfolk, including older girls of larger families, were settling the smaller children into their bunks for the night.

Lil took out a flask of her favourite

imported whiskey and offered it. Both her new friends took the merest cautious sip. Honesty spluttered some, confirming Lil's guess that the pair were as unfamiliar with spirits as she'd expected but not averse to experimentation outside the purview of their respective fathers.

She took a more generous swig herself. She savoured the taste of the fine liquor while its warmth seemed to spread and ease out the kinks and aches from her arms and legs.

It was still and peaceful round the wagon train. From afar, across the scrub, came the howl of a coyote. It was answered once, from a yet further distance. Then silence returned till a breath of wind ruffled the white canvas tops of the wagons. For a moment, the name prairie schooner seemed more perfectly apt. In Lil's imagination, the wagons could have been a fleet of picture-book ships straining at anchors, ready to move out across a dark, rustling sea that was really grass.

Unbeknowing of Lil's long-held adoration of Jackson Farraday, Honesty let slip her own preoccupation with the manly attractions of the new guide. The loosening of her tongue might also have been added confirmation of her head's unfamiliarity with hard drink.

'Oh my, isn't Jackson Farraday the most handsome fellow, Lil?'

Lil said a mite scoffingly, 'Ain't fell for him, have you?'

'What if I have?'

'We-ell, you're no bad picker, but Jackson is a born man of the frontier, not of your kind at all in point of fact. This is no country for you.'

'Mister Farraday is too much man for me, is that what you really mean?'

Lil shook her head. She didn't want an upset with Honesty but knew what she'd said was true, notwithstanding any potential rivalry in the matter of winning Jackson's attention.

'It's just that I thought you were Luke Reiner's girl,' she said. 'Don't care for him myself, but I figured he had your pa's nod to court you, and he came with you folks from back East.'

Honesty pouted. 'Luke has nothing but expectations. He told me buying a saddle mount and equipping himself for our journey cleaned him out.'

'Then how come your father sees his suit as fitting?'

'Luke told him he has a cousin in California. When we get there, he'll be provided family money to invest in good farming land . . . Pa was happy with his guarantees. Besides, I hadn't seen Jackson Farraday then.'

Prudence's ample body seemed to swell as she took in a deep breath. She tutted primly.

'You should be careful. My father has warned me about the evil that's in the hearts of all men, but especially those who've not come to the Lord.'

Lil reflected silently that fights weren't likely to break out over the affections of Prudence, even in territory where young spinsters were in demand. Though robustly healthy in looks, her physique was that associated with women of maturer years. The best that might be said of Prudence's fuller figure was that its like appealed to painters of the Rubens school.

Prudence hadn't finished admonishing her daintier friend.

'Father also considers you a bad influence on me — you know how he tries to discourage our friendship. You think too much about men, Honesty. And as for forsaking Mister Reiner for a new beau, aren't you forgetting his secret present you wear so close to your heart?'

The notion of having secrets never sat well with Lil; she maintained so few of her own.

'A present? What is it?'

'Show her, Honesty,' Prudence said sternly.

'I will!'

Far from being reluctant, Honesty unbuttoned the top of her dress with an air of defiance. She fished out an oval locket. Between two and three inches high and about one and three-fourths of an inch wide, it was suspended on a silver chain about fourteen inches long.

'See, Lil? And it has his silly picture in it!'

She reached behind her slim white neck and unhooked the delicately linked chain. The hinged, chased top of the locket swung to the side to show the photographic portrait of Luke Reiner, stiffly posed.

Prudence snorted derisively, not a very feminine sound and not very kind.

Whereupon Honesty impetuously flung the trinket into a nearby patch of brush.

'I've done with the gew-gaw, Pru! Him to boot! He made a fool of himself in Silver Vein, and I can't abide association with a loser. I'll wear his tag around my neck no more!'

Prudence smiled in sly satisfaction. 'Yes, good riddance to his silly pendant. You'll be better off without him, too. Without any of these rough men to be honest. They're just the same — trash.'

'Hmmm,' Lil said, dubious. 'As long

as you're sure it's right to throw away what might've cost good dollars.'

Honesty said brightly, 'Let's talk about something else now, shall we?'

They did, but later, when all the camp was sleeping, Lil came back. She sought and found the locket and chain, well-hidden in the brush but a small, uncovered part giving off tell-tale glitter in the moonlight.

She retrieved it, returned to her blankets and tucked it into one of her saddlebags.

There was no knowing just when or how much Reiner's discarded gift might be of use, was there?

5

Riding the Currents

Jackson woke with the feel of someone shaking his arm. One minute he was fast asleep; the next wide awake, alert. Such was the nature of a man attuned to his surroundings by a life spent outdoors, often on dangerous trails.

'Wha' the — ?

'It's me — Honesty. I came to find you.'

Jackson had come to an instant and full possession of his senses. He also knew his waker must have lost hers.

'Shh! You mustn't wake the camp,' he warned.

It was dark and quiet, but not completely. Below where he was settled on a grassy bank under the stars a short distance from the circled wagons, a creek gurgled along. A night breeze blew, carrying the scents of dying cookfires, the party's livestock and crushed bluestem.

'No, of course not,' she said in no way deterred by his frosty tone.

'What do you want, Miss Petrie?'

She swallowed. 'Haven't we gotten something else we could do other than sleep alone and cold?'

'You know damn well we haven't, you little minx!' he hissed. 'Of all the lame-brained notions . . . I oughta tell your father! What do you think you're playing at? You need your butt paddled!'

She tried to make light of his reprimand. 'Oh, that would be nice! It could be noisy though, couldn't it?'

'Shut up! Get away from me, will you? Go back to your wagon!'

'Then we'd both have to carry on being cold and lonely.'

'For God's sake . . . be reasonable!'

'Oh, I thought you'd understand. These things just happen. I can't help it.'

He groaned. 'What do you think your

father would do if he knew where you were? Or Luke Reiner? It's enough to have him scowling at me every time he catches you giving me the eye! You must be crazy.'

Her eyes filled with tears, but whether they were anger or sorrow he couldn't tell.

'Luke Reiner just — bothers me now. But I'm not minded to talk about that. It would spoil what we have.'

'You're dreaming, young lady. We have nothing. Do I have to say it again?' He was emphatic as he could be without raising his voice above an urgent whisper. '*Get your ass outa here!*'

The girl flinched. For what was like several seconds, she continued to look at him with the plea in her glistening eyes, but she could think of nothing more to say. Her rash overture rejected, she turned and crept away, her bare feet rustling a dragged-out, fading lament in the grass.

Afterwards, Jackson closed his eyes

and tried to forget it had happened. He put it down to the silliness of her youth and a possibly inadequate upbringing with a mother either dead or run away . . . not in evidence, anyway. Complete orphans were not uncommon in his world, but coincidentally his life already had in it a similarly placed girl — Lilian Goodnight — though she'd never pulled any stunt on him as brazen as Honesty Petrie's.

Why did he have to attract such motherless young women? Was it part of the price a man had to pay for being competent at the skills called for in a true Westerner?

Another thought that came in the disturbed peace of the starry night concerned Luke Reiner. It was not the first time it had been an irritation on the edges of his awareness.

Maybe assumption by Reiner that the nubile Honesty would be his in California was all it needed to keep the sham scout riding with Petrie's party, regardless of his public trouncing in

Silver Vein. But somehow — pretty and untouched though the filly was — Jackson didn't think following a girl so obviously naïve, so immature, could be motive enough for a grown man he figured to be thoroughly wise in the ways of the world.

★   ★   ★

Misfit Lil, too, had noted the increasingly black looks Luke Reiner was giving Jackson Farraday. He probably didn't know his girl — or the one he thought was spoken for in his name — no longer wore his pendant next to her creamy skin. Yet no one missed the longing glances she saved for Jackson alone.

Lil had a premonition which she preferred to call a hunch, because a hunch didn't sound so scary. And it wasn't a fear Honesty Petrie might become a rival for Jackson's interest. She'd known Jackson long enough to know that he wouldn't lose his head over a pretty girl who threw herself at it. No, she'd became convinced Honesty Petrie was going to end up making big trouble for Jackson.

It was time for some straight, girl-to-girl talking in private.

Jackson had led the wagon train a creditable twenty miles in one day to a campsite on a thickly grassed meadow that sloped down to the wooded banks of a broad mountain stream. The timber gave shelter to pools along the edge of the watercourse that were fine spots for washing and swimming.

Lil caught sight of Honesty and Prudence making for a beached cove she knew was situated a few hundred yards away from the camped wagons. They carried towels and she surmised they were looking for privacy.

No better opportunity might come up. What Lil had to say could safely be said in front of Prudence. The big, solid girl was a reverend's daughter and Honesty's closest friend. She wasn't gossipy. Contrariwise, she was quiet and a tad secretive.

Lil followed circumspectly, not showing herself.

She came to a pause in a colony of aspens, deciding it would be best to let the girls complete their ablutions before confronting them as though coming upon them unawares, perhaps as they made their return.

A breeze stirred the leaves over her head, making them quiver, and she settled to wait. In fall, the trees would be beautiful, all tints of red and yellow. Now, their leaves were green, very big and rounded with sawteeth on their edges. She wondered where the people of the wagon train would be by the time the leaves' change of colour was upon them; what would she and Jackson be doing . . . Who would be dead; who would be living.

The sound of laughter and excited feminine voices drifted to her. She couldn't distinguish words due to the rustle of the aspens. Finally, though she told herself she didn't really want to eavesdrop, she crept closer to the girls. After all, they were taking an exceptionally long time to do whatever they had to do.

She paused behind the screen of a thicket of bulrushes and listened.

What she heard first was not words but a series of tiny, inarticulate cries. Then . . .

'*Ah!*'

The sound of a short, breathy sigh both increased her puzzlement and gave her a clue.

She knew very well that curiosity was inherent and spontaneous in others just as it was in herself. It belonged to the condition of late girlhood, whatever attempts were made by elders to repress it. Past near-daredevil behaviour in her own life had been a manifestation of the very same. It had brought her disgrace and expulsion from a finishing school in Boston, Massachusetts, where she'd been dispatched by her misguided father to learn the decorum and ladylike accomplishments for which instruction hadn't been available to a tomboy ranch-girl in Utah.

The sigh was followed by a gasp and a second sigh that was more drawn out, and deeper.

'*Ahhh!* You angel!'

Lil heard a giggle from Honesty.

'A sinful angel! Oh, Prudence, you naughty girl! You've made my face all wet. What would your pa the parson say?'

Prudence said breathlessly, 'He need never know because we shall follow the Eleventh Commandment.'

'Eleventh? I thought there were only ten.'

'I'm funning, you noodle. The Eleventh Commandment is 'Thou shalt never be found out.''

Lil pushed through the tangle of bulrushes.

The two girls were by the water's edge, rising from their spread towels. Their outer clothes were draped over bushes a short way off. Stockings and undergarments were in neat little piles where they couldn't be splashed from the stream.

'Let's go have another wash,' Honesty said to her companion.

'Hullo there!' Lil said. She wasn't in the least embarrassed to see the pair in a state of nature.

Prudence's hands flew to cover parts of her ample self. But what was left confirmed and accentuated Lil's impression that she had the kind of pelvis generously designed for child-bearing and associated activities.

Honesty, running to the water, stopped and swung round to face her. She smiled shyly, which surprised Lil, but she didn't bother to try concealing her perky, high, round breasts or anything else.

'Oh, my goodness, you've surprised us jaybird-naked! What must you think?'

'Nothing of it,' Lil said.

She had long subscribed to the belief that there could be no great sin in nakedness, nor in satisfying the natural desires of the flesh and enjoying to the full the delicious sensations for which a benevolent Creator had efficiently designed his living creatures.

'What did you see?'

Again, Lil said, 'Nothing. Nothing I mind at all.'

Her sympathy was with the girls. She'd hated the atmosphere she'd found exemplified by her classmates in Boston. In the East, young women — probably young men, too — were racked by ridiculous feelings of guilt about their bodies and their natural urges. Those who'd had no rural background whatsoever had seemed to be in a state of blind ignorance about life and how the various species, including humans, survived.

Lil, with the help of a willing gardener's-boy, had made it her mission to re-educate them after lights-out. She'd refused to accept the absurd notion that relations between consenting adults had to be only as sanctioned by authoritarian parents and preacher-men.

'Nothing, eh?' Honesty said, walking back with a mischievous lilt to her voice. 'Then you must join us and help keep our secrets, you funny, lovely girl! Mustn't she, Prudence?'

Whereupon she flung herself at Lil plucking at the strings and buttons of her buckskins. With the hefty Prudence promptly helping to restrain any possible opposition, Lil was overpowered.

She didn't try to resist.

'Hey! What do you think you're doing?'

It was an unnecessary question. It was very obvious what the two girls were doing and they didn't bother to give Lil an answer. Honesty's small fingers were nimble and sharp. Lil's mannish duds were quickly peeled off and she found herself as obviously female as them.

They took her hands and ran as a trio into the water, laughing and happy.

'Let's be the nymphs of the stream!' Honesty cried joyously.

Lil couldn't bring herself to dislike the girl, however big an objectionable fool she'd made of herself with first Reiner and now Jackson. And it was scarcely an appropriate moment to launch into a warning lecture about the trouble Honesty was storing up for herself with her flirting games.

Together with a straight-cut fringe, Honesty's distinctive pigtails framed her face, reaching to her shoulders. But it was the eyes that impressed Lil; she warmed sympathetically to the half-humorous curiosity she fancied she found in them. Honesty's eyes surely looked out on a world she found exciting, novel and waiting to be explored.

They waded out till they were waist high in the pool. Both wagon train girls then proved themselves to be adequate swimmers, though neither was as practised as Lil.

The faster-running water out in the stream hadn't been warmed by the sun. Snow-fed from the mountains, it was cool, refreshing, exhilarating.

Lil dived under the surface into its

clear depths, imitating an otter and enjoying herself with her acrobatics till she finally had to come up for air. This was the life!

Honesty and Prudence, who stood watching from where the water was knee-deep, were overawed by her athleticism in the water. They clapped delightedly at the show the 'wild girl' put on for them.

Eventually, they waded back to the stream bank, their clothes and the emigrant girls' towels. The sun would soon die behind the mountains and it would turn cold.

'Come on, let's go back to the camp,' Prudence said. 'We should be helping get supper.'

The vigorous exercise had lifted all their cares for a while and Lil didn't choose to break the relaxed mood.

Only later did she realize she'd failed. She'd been subverted from her purpose by the girls' tomfoolery. She hadn't delivered the all-important warning to Honesty about her rash behaviour.

6

Jackson Rides into Trouble

Several days later, the wagon train was trekking across high, barren ground where a stiff wind blew off the snow-tipped peaks of the Henry Mountains. The country was very rugged and dry. Though their route now trended west and well as south, it was not the one Jackson Farraday would have chosen. The roads at higher elevations could be impassable due to rockslides and snow. Bull Creek Pass was usually blocked by snowdrifts until late July. But that particular die had been cast before he'd joined the Petrie party — cast by Luke Reiner.

Earlier, Jackson had sat round a camp fire with Winton Petrie, the Reverend James Hannigan and Reiner.

The incompetent trailsman had sketched a map with a stick in the dirt.

'See? There's this town here — Buzzard City. We should head there.'

Jackson murmured, 'A dreary place, Reiner. I figure it'll be a ghost town before long.'

'But we can replenish stores there,' Reiner said.

Petrie backed him.

'It'll be a chance to stock up. The families are short of rations. I hear they're badmouthing me as leader because oil for their lamps is getting low. Yours is a good plan, Reiner.'

Hannigan quoted piously, 'Behold, how good and how pleasant it is for brethren to dwell together in unity!'

But Jackson thought it out-of-character for Reiner to be showing such consideration for his charges. The bogus guide wouldn't be able to buy much himself in any hick town. Jackson had heard it gossiped that Reiner was heading for California without a red cent to his name.

He compromised. 'I'd advise we veer southerly apiece rather than pass directly through Buzzard City. The folks there are generally poor and will ask high prices for what they can sell to strangers. Maybe one of two of the men can ride in and buy whatever's absolutely necessary. The wagons can stay out of sight by the river that's here.'

He made his own marks on the map.

'We'll also need to refill the water kegs by then.'

Reiner's mouth tightened.

'Obliged for the opinion, but we'll need grub,' he said adamantly.

Jackson shrugged. 'You can use a rifle, can't you? There's deer hereabouts . . . pheasant, snipe and quail to boot. Or if your taste doesn't run to game birds, maybe you'd consider cottontail and jackrabbits.'

Petrie reflected. He rubbed the back of his balding head and said in judgement, 'Mister Farraday has raised sensible points.'

Reiner grunted before lapsing into

stony silence, and so it had been decided, though with bad grace on the one part. Reiner had tossed aside the stick with which he'd outlined his proposed route in unspoken disgust.

Jackson also remembered now the strange scars he'd noted on Reiner's wrists as he'd used the stick. Out west, a man's past life was his own business and nobody else's. He was free to start over if that was what he wanted. Many folks joined wagon trains to put old lives behind them, trying to forget. Others brought their secrets with them, prepared to fight to protect them. Jackson wondered if the wrist scars were matched by others on Reiner's ankles.

Could Reiner be an ex-convict? Could the marks have been caused by the irons worn when a man was put to work on a penitentiary's chain gang?

Again, Jackson asked himself what Reiner's game might truly be. Whole wagon trains had been tricked by rogues before.

Famously, Alexander Fancher and his wagon train had left Fort Smith, Arkansas, for California, only to be attacked in southwestern Utah by Indians. With fifty men, forty women and fifty children under his leadership, Fancher had circled the wagons and mounted a stiff and successful defence. Then Mormons had approached the camp and offered to lead the emigrants to safety. But it had been a trick. The Mormons had sided with the Indians.

The Mormon militia had shot down the men; the women and children had been left to the Indians. Only seventeen infants had been spared. Eventually, Indian agent John D. Lee, a Mormon leader, had been executed for his role in the affair.

But the Mountain Meadows Massacre was now more than twenty years back. Was it in any way possible Luke Reiner could be involved in like treachery today?

Jackson didn't expect large-scale

Indian or religious troubles, but pre-arranged hijacking and looting crossed his mind. The emigrants brought all their worldly goods in their wagons apart from what they'd cashed up. Good pickings . . .

Some of the lumbering prairie schooners carried loads of up to 2,500 pounds, which was 900 more than the recommended limit. Besides the young and the elderly infirm, the wagons' freight was food supplies, cooking utensils, water kegs, tools and implements, bedding, clothing and items of prized furniture that hadn't already been abandoned on the arduous trip.

That day, rockslides forced several detours for the cumbersome rigs, but Jackson at last brought them safely to a patch of semi-alpine grassland through which a river flowed, fringed by a variety of timber.

Jackson signalled the halt for the night and waited for the others to catch up.

'Roll them wagons in, fellers!' he

hollered, and pointed the way to a convenient flat dotted with woods.

A flock of black-capped chickadees vocalized the threat they perceived in the arrivals. Their complex, four-note alarm cry — *chicka-dee-dee-dee* — sounded as they rose from the denser treetops, a giant's handful of specks thrown across an orange-pink sky.

'This place is like a slice of Heaven, isn't it?' Honesty exclaimed from the seat of the Petrie wagon.

Luke Reiner, riding past, chose to take it as a comment to himself, maybe to tease him for being in a sour mood.

'Never one for Scripture-talk, honey. Heaven's just a word. Ain't no God out here.'

'Well, it could be I wasn't addressing you, Luke.'

The Reverend James Hannigan also happened to overhear the exchange.

'God is always with the righteous, sir!'

★ ★ ★

Jackson was watching Luke Reiner day and night. He'd noticed how keen the man was to see Buzzard City. When darkness came, he was therefore on hand to see him saddle up and head out of camp on a vague dirt trail that wended in the direction of the dreary little town and its long-abandoned gold diggings.

He followed, fixing to track Reiner by the light of a rising moon, but was forced to hang back because he didn't want to be seen and cover was sparse. It was poor land where Reiner was headed — growth consisted in the main of salt-desert shrubs, blackbrush, and galleta grass.

Eventually and abruptly, the trail hit thicker vegetation. Simultaneously, by an unfortunate quirk of fate, the moon vanished behind thick, black cloud. In a stretch of woodland that included piñon trees interspersed with juniper, Jackson lost his quarry.

He said, disgusted, 'Damn!' and got down from his horse. Tracks were hard to see, if they were there. Striking a match gave no help. Small, disturbed rodents scuttled away through the scrub. A rattlesnake slid across the rocks that dimly passed here for the trail.

His horse, momentarily left to its own devices, moved through screening vegetation toward a waterhole. A light mist seeped up from the undergrowth and clung to the treetops. When the horse was almost to the beckoning drink, followed by Jackson, it whinnied and pranced. Too late, Jackson caught the smell of other horseflesh in among the bushes.

He never saw his attacker, but assumed it was Reiner who, despite the care he'd taken, must have spotted him and waited in ambush. He swivelled round, his arm coming up in instinctive defence.

Before Jackson saw anything, or heard more than the pounding crunch of approaching footsteps, an iron hardness slammed into the side of his head.

An explosion of blinding stars robbed him of his senses and pitched him into black emptiness.

★　★　★

Jackson Farraday was missing. Rising from her blankets at first light, as was her custom, Misfit Lil quickly discovered he was nowhere in camp. That seemed inexplicable, but there could be an innocuous explanation.

Nonetheless, she felt her heart skip a beat and her mouth turned suddenly dry.

Disquiet turned to alarm when Jackson's horse wandered in, saddled but riderless. Her immediate conclusion was he must have gone riding sometime in the night, or before dawn, and taken a fall.

'Reiner! You seen your boss?' she demanded of the surly scout.

'He ain't my boss, should you happen to mean Farraday. We're appointed jointly. And no, I ain't seen him. Not since yesterday.'

Lil had noticed Reiner himself had been absent from the camp.

'Where were you last evening?' she challenged.

The reply came with the glibness of a smart mouth giving a prepared answer.

'I rode to Buzzard City, to taste liquor and mix with sociable comp'ny in a real saloon.'

Lil's eyes narrowed. She knew something of the dispute concerning the wagon train's choice of trails and stopping places. Like Jackson, she also had yet to figure what reason had led Luke Reiner to guide the party where he had.

'You sure Jackson didn't tag along to town with you?' she asked.

'Just said not, didn't I? Ain't seen him since yesterday.'

Faced with his clipped animosity, Lil knew she'd get no more out of him . . . lies or truth. A cold anger and an overpowering desire to wipe the smirk off Reiner's face gripped her.

With difficulty, she mastered it. Anger and defiance would take her nowhere, though they might surprise a man who plainly was used to girls who didn't have the courage to question what he told them.

She repeated softly, sceptically, 'Since yesterday . . . '

She didn't like it at all. Jackson had gone missing during the hours of full dark and might be lying injured somewhere, in need of help.

' . . . Then maybe someone better run along and take a look for him, huh?'

Reiner shrugged his blocky shoulders. 'Suit yourself, gal. I don't give a damn.'

The most urgent job was to go find Jackson. Heart pounding, blood beating against her temples, Lil left Reiner, went and readied Rebel and set out tracking.

She heeled her horse forward slowly at first, circling, but the only fresh signs leading out of the camp went in the one direction — where Buzzard City lay.

She rode ahead at a low, easy lope, looking into the distance. She was an accomplished horsewoman and she'd trained her mount herself from a foal. The rugged, desolate terrain of the high country failed to deter them as they followed the little-used trail.

Timberwolves might be watching them from a stand of spruce or ponderosa pine. A mountain lion could lurk in a jumble of rocks . . . lions did dwell in the Henry Mountains and were encountered by lone travellers on rare occasions. But Lil thought only of Jackson Farraday, someplace out here, hurt or dying.

After lengthy minutes, a small puff of dust thrown up by a dark, moving speck against harshly eroded rock gave her cause for hope. Something, someone was coming to meet her.

Pleasure lit up her face when she drew close enough to recognize it was Jackson! Her smile and her relief faded when she saw his paleness and that blood stained one side of his long, sun-bleached hair. His unsteady gait suggested he was dazed.

'Oh, Jackson!' she cried. 'What happened?'

'Bushwhacked, I guess,' he said grimly. He sat himself on a handy-sized rock.

Lil jumped down and soaked a kerchief with water from her canteen. Gently, she wiped his blood- and dirt-caked head and face while he drank.

'Where were you going?'

'I was following Luke Reiner. I figured he was heading for Buzzard City and thought someone should know what he did when he got there. I was ambushed.'

'By Reiner?'

'That I can't swear to. I lost him going through some woods in the dark and got down. Someone was waiting there though. They didn't like me or what I was doing.'

'It must've been Reiner!' Lil said fiercely. 'The filthy polecat! He's been waiting his chance since the set-to in Silver Vein. And Honesty making up to you hasn't helped none either. Petrie must dismiss the scoundrel for this.'

Jackson shook his head. 'But I've not a jot of proof against the man, just suspicion.'

'This is a sorry story to hear. You know it was Reiner!'

'If it was Reiner, the whys confound me. I don't think he could really have been fixing on squaring his beating. Maybe what he wanted was to stop me seeing where he went and what he did there.'

Lil thought about it.

'That may figure. Reiner's not the kind to let settling a grudge get the better of his cunning. What *is* he up to?'

'Maybe we'll find out when we get to camp.'

★ ★ ★

They didn't. When they reached the circle of wagons, they found the emigrants in a state of distraction. That Jackson Farraday, their principal guide, had gone absent overnight concerned no one. Someone else was also missing.

Lambasted by Winton Petrie, everyone was anxiously seeking answers to a new question.

Where was Honesty Petrie?

7

'A Murderer Loose . . .'

The entire party had been recruited into the search for the wagonmaster's missing daughter. Even Luke Reiner seemed to be doing all he could to demonstrate an enthusiasm to find the girl in apparent disregard of her recent spurning of him.

'That gal was promised me. It was all right by her pa,' he said.

'Is that so?' Lil questioned insolently. 'I thought she'd turned her attentions elsewhere.'

Reiner caught her drift. He swung on Jackson.

'You better not have had a hand in this disappearing, Farraday,' he warned.

'How could I? You left me stunned and horseless out on the trail.'

'I don't know what you're talking

about!' Reiner snapped back. 'I heard you been seeing her on the sly — pestering her.'

Lil and Jackson let the unwarranted charge lie. Nobody was much interested in what sounded like a petty quarrel in comparison to the pressing mystery of what had become of Honesty Petrie.

The blow to his head and his subsequent walk had left Jackson so weary and aching he could hardly move, but with a bandage round his head like a turban, he insisted on joining Lil in the search.

The land slanted into some willow bottoms and to the edge of a narrow, winding river. Overhead two buzzards soared on rigid wings, riding the wind. Open spaces broke the trees and the searchers beat the tall grass. Lil and Jackson met a group that included Prudence Hannigan.

Lil was shocked to see Prudence's obvious distress. Prudence had never been any striking beauty, full of the joy of life, but today she was pale and shaking rather than stolid and sulky as she usually was in the presence of elders.

Unintentionally, Lil found herself comparing the two emigrant girls. They were striking when seen together because they were complete contrasts — on the surface. Evidently, Prudence feared something bad had befallen her dainty, vivacious friend.

'Don't worry, Prudence,' Lil said. 'She can't be far away. We'll find her.'

But Lil was deeply worried herself. She shivered in anticipation of an unpleasant outcome, and everyone's fears were confirmed in short order.

Honesty Petrie was discovered face down in the shallows of the river. She was naked and dead.

* * *

'Drowned, by God!' a man said.

The word was quickly spread that Honesty was found. A wail of shock and grief followed. A horse was called for and fetched; the body draped gently across it.

Nobody could understand, not even Lil. She'd seen for herself that Honesty was a moderately competent swimmer and was not so rash that she would have bathed in a manner apt to lead her into difficulty. Also, her clothes were not found gently folded some place on the river bank, but sodden and scattered further along it as though they'd been thrown into the stream to be carried away.

Then a man with a modicum of medical training said Honesty hadn't died by drowning. She'd taken in too little water.

'I reckon it only looks like a drowning — that we're assuming she was drowned when she wasn't. My conclusion is she was smothered — suffocated — during the night or shortly after daybreak.'

'Murder!' someone said.

The cry was taken up and enlarged upon. It was claimed Honesty and her clothes had been thrown into the river in a panicky attempt to dispose of the evidence of a dastardly crime. The circumstances allowed no other explanation . . .

Indignation and conjecture took a noisy hold.

Jackson called for calm. 'Some dignity, folks! A life has been lost here. A young lady of our party has been taken from us and we must show respect.'

In due course, after two of the older women had prepared the body for burial, the chastened emigrants took Honesty on her last ride; to her last resting place. A spot in a cedar grove was chosen for her by her ashen, trembling father.

Shovels struck the hard dirt. They dug the grave deep.

Lil noted Prudence was absent from the interment. It was no wonder, she thought. The girls had been the closest of friends and Honesty's sudden, violent loss must be heartbreaking.

A distressed woman confided in a whisper, 'Poor girl. They do tell she's collapsed through shock an's confined to her bunk in the parson's wagon.'

But brought out from the same wagon for the occasion was the Hannigans' cabinet organ. Smaller and weighing tolerably less than a piano or a church's pipe organ, it was easier to transport, less prone to damage where good roads were non-existent. It was a reed instrument with a foot-operated vacuum bellows and a keyboard.

The organ was played by Hannigan's wife, Mabel, a drab woman with faded eyes in a prematurely much-lined face. She struck up with what was announced as Honesty's favourite hymn, *What a Friend We Have in Jesus*.

Lil was powerfully affected by the melancholy in the strains of the organ, the untrained voices and the sigh of the breeze that whipped them away. When the congregation reached the second verse, there was scarcely a dry eye.

Have we trials and temptations?
Is there trouble anywhere?
We should never be discouraged;
take it to the Lord in prayer.
Can we find a friend so faithful
who will all our sorrows share?
Jesus knows our every weakness;
take it to the Lord in prayer.

Solemn words were spoken over the body by the Reverend James Hannigan.

'Almighty God, we thank you for the life of your child Honesty and for all that you have given us through her and her innocence. And we thank you that in mercy you have delivered her from the miseries of this sinful life . . . '

Lil didn't listen to Hannigan's droning, but to her own heart.

Honesty's had been the 'innocence' you met in a big-eyed kitten that nonetheless had claws which could scratch and tear, doing damage inadvertently, playfully. It was painful having to accept that Honesty, however pesky, was gone. For ever . . .

It had all taken place so quickly and unexpectedly. But who had killed her, and why?

Lil knew the questions would not be laid to rest as quickly as her still-pretty remains, which were lowered into the deep hole in the ground.

After the ceremony and the departure of most of the attending emigrants, they shovelled in the dirt. Six men took turns in pairs, and they piled the biggest rocks they could find on the mound and around it.

A headboard was fashioned from a tabletop donated from among a family's stock of furniture. The stuff was proving heavy and taking up a lot of wagon space. Marking Honesty's grave was a worthier use. Her name and birth and death dates were burned into the wood with a hot iron.

Lil wondered sadly how long it would last in the weather of the mountain wilderness.

★   ★   ★

Death was habitually cruel, swift and unexpected on the overland trails. Drownings stopped many from reaching their promised land. It was the second major cause of death after accidental shootings. Lil had once read that more than 300 people had died from drowning between 1840 and 1860. Nineteen emigrants had met their death crossing the River Platte near Fort Laramie in 1849. In one incident at North Fork the next year, forty-nine emigrants had drowned.

But Honesty's death hadn't been like that, it sounded. Before she was cold in the grave, the wagon train was demanding an explanation.

'How did this happen? The river was considered free of hazards for bathers . . . '

'Miss Petrie was a capable swimm– '

'Shuddup, Clinton! We bin told it was no accident.'

'What was she doing out there in the dark?'

'I hear the body had bruises . . . '

'My daughter was killed,' Winton Petrie said, addressing a full assembly of his party. 'I figure there's a murderer on the loose among us and he must be brought to account!'

A sudden sense of unease gripped Lil. If she'd ever thought she was travelling with the merest bunch of knock-kneed town-dwellers from back East, the outrage she could feel consuming those about her disabused any notion that they would not take stern and ruthless action against the person responsible for Honesty's death.

Foul play would be punished; the wagon train would be purged.

To Lil's immediate horror, Luke Reiner, also judging the prevailing mood, seized his chance.

It was high time to settle the score; to wipe out his rival. Westerners, Easterners . . . no one had mercy on a man who had his way with a female, forcing her, killing her.

'Who was unaccounted for last night?' he asked shrewdly. 'Which man wasn't by his woman's side, or missing from his blankets?'

Lil could see what was coming. She couldn't hold her tongue.

'I know who you're trying to blacken!' she cried. 'But it's a lie. Mister Farraday was lying injured out on the trail to Buzzard City. You know that better than anyone!'

'Know no such thing, missy,' Reiner scoffed. 'You're out of line. I went to Buzzard City, sure. I didn't have no riverside trysts, like a certain gent who came back after daylight, feigning injury — the said result of a 'maginary dry-gulching!'

Farraday got to his feet and spoke up. 'Talk plain, Reiner!'

'Thought I had, Longhair. You been sweet-talking Miss Petrie ever since we left Silver Vein, turning her head 'cause you knowed she was promised to me and you weren't content with taking my job.'

'Hogwash!'

'Yeah, mebbe it is. Mebbe you jest

wanted to get inta her drawers, you dirty skunk!'

Gasps of anger and shock rippled through the gathering around the big camp fire.

'I swear I never made any approaches to the girl!' Farraday said, his eyes blazing with anger. 'I'm telling the truth. Who says otherwise?'

There was a second's breathless silence, then the Reverend James Hannigan coughed and climbed to his feet.

'Sir, I don't think it wholly insignificant my daughter has reported Miss Petrie was indeed much taken with your handsome looks. And Miss Petrie claimed the feeling was reciprocated.'

Jackson shook his head in disbelief.

'I'm afraid the girls must've been romancing about me, Reverend. Or maybe the death of her friend has started your daughter imagining things never done or said.'

'No, sir!' Hannigan insisted hotly. 'Moreover, Prudence has told me Miss

Petrie went to you privately one night when you camped apiece from the wagons. It was seen!'

A murmur of consternation greeted the parson's testimony.

Jackson was momentarily flummoxed, but he recovered in an instant. His tone of voice conveyed his affront

'And I sent her away, Reverend! It was nothing. Her visit was silly childishness instigated by herself. On my oath, I took no advantage!'

But Reiner, seeing the knife had been stuck in, proceeded to twist it.

'He's lying through his teeth, the bastard! What else would he do? I see it this way. He arranged to meet my Honesty by the river. When she resisted his attentions, he molested her and stilled her tongue 'bout his foulness for all time. He chucked her clothes and her ravished body into the water, not knowing they'd be washed up in the shallows.'

'By God, the lies are all yours, Reiner!'

'Brethren!' Hannigan roared. 'There'll be no blasphemy! In the fullness of time, all must come before the Almighty and face His judgement, but this awful business must be placed before a temporal court of justice.'

Lil could keep quiet no longer.

'Don't make a fool of yourself, Reverend! There are no proper courthouses in the frontier districts and judges ride their circuits with as much regard for mob law as federal law. Who will try the case, and when?'

Lil was only stating what was well known to the average westerner. Although better trained in specific points of law than local peace officers, travelling judges tended to be almost as informal.

They based their decisions on common sense more often than on strict interpretation of the law. Overworked, some were known to let financial considerations — in short, bribes — sway them in performance of their duties. Moreover, honest jurors were hard to find and in the wilder, more primitive communities held troublemakers and outlaw gangs in high esteem.

But Lil's argument sounded like disrespect to the parson. Women, especially young women, weren't expected to meddle in matters of import; of life and death.

Her outspokenness didn't help Jackson's position. He was a virtual stranger to the emigrants, and he stood accused by one less apart from them and who ostensibly shared their dreams and aspirations.

Winton Petrie's reason and sense of fairness were clouded by his grief. He seized the chance to vent his vibrant anger.

'Hold your tongue, girl! This party is sick to the back teeth of your for'ardness! You're rude and uninvited. 'Tain't natural in a female! And you've no say in the matter. Your betters and elders will do the deciding.'

Lil found herself subjected to the unappreciative wagoners' glares. Worried, maybe frightened by the notion of a killer in their ranks, they accepted their leader's condemnation.

'Yeah, we've put up with a damned lot,' came a muttered protest.

'The hell with the pair of 'em! They ain't runnin' this shebang.'

General feelings of inferiority to and disgruntlement with the trail-savvy pair did the rest.

'It's settled,' Petrie said. 'Jackson Farraday will be placed under restraint, to be turned over to the law in Buzzard City. The spot where my daughter was murdered is close enough inside the town's jurisdiction. It's plain enough — a trial must be held someplace; justice must be done.'

A sober murmur approved the wagonmaster's announcement. Jackson was ringed by burly male emigrants, every one of them armed. The option to break and run didn't exist.

Lil laughed inwardly and mirthlessly. The truth would hit Petrie and his ignorant followers like a ton bull digging in its hoofs on the end of a hard-and-fast rope. The workings of justice in the scattered settlements of southern Utah were erratic and uncertain. Any trial that could be staged in short order in Buzzard City would be a farce.

Then Luke Reiner intervened, and for once Lil could agree with him.

'Now let's not be hasty, Winton. Buzzard City ain't nothing more'n a hick town.'

He turned to the Reverend Hannigan, aiming to encompass his approval. 'It's a den of sinners, Reverend. Outlaw scum and the like, lying low from God-fearing fellow-men and the rule of law. You folks should stay clear of the dump.'

Lil said, 'True, Reiner. Howsoever, ain't this a suspicious change of your tune? Didn't you want the wagon train to come thisaway?'

Reiner didn't like to be reminded. His face went red and he scowled.

'You can't talk to me that way, kid! Keep your nose outa this! Murder's been done. We need to quit the shilly-shallying and hold our own trial. Then we hang the murderer ourselfs and move on fast. We've got to get across them deserts afore summer makes 'em an oven!'

As Reiner's motive in dismissing Buzzard City became apparent, dismay clutched at Lil's heart.

Lynch law!

Who had really killed Honesty? How could she rescue Jackson from such a dangerous situation?

8

Lil under Fire

Lil was a lone voice, speaking up for her friend and reluctant hero. No one was willing to believe Jackson Farraday could be innocent. She could only guess at how long it would be before Reiner's blunt recommendations and the implacability of their outraged leaders would persuade the wagon train folk to screw up their courage and put Jackson to summary, ugly death.

She put it to the agitated crowd that Reiner, too, had gone absent some time after camp was pitched at dusk.

'He could've just as easily as Mister Farraday been guilty of Honesty's killing during the night. Maybe he's trying to throw us off with his accusing. Mightn't that be the way a real murderer would work?'

Reiner had been growing increasingly excited, stimulated by the mood of the party. A mob mentality was surely brewing. His eyes were uncommonly bright. Light caught beads of sweat on his brow and his upper lip.

'Don't listen to the bitch!' he snapped. 'She can't prove a thing on me. I wasn't here, but ever'body *knows* where I went. I rode to Buzzard City to taste liquor in the saloon thar. I was witnessed back at the wagons inside a coupla hours. I could get a half-dozen men here to swear it.'

Lil persisted. 'Just an hour would've been long enough. Does anyone know when Honesty vanished?'

Despite some foot shuffling, no one answered except Reiner.

'She's crazy! I got no reason fer killing Miss Petrie. We was good as engaged to be married in California where a fortune waits me. Her pa had given his say-so fer me to court her.'

Winton Petrie made no attempt to deny his contention.

116

Outnumbered and apparently out-argued, Lil was forced to contain herself.

Most people mistook her silence. They thought she'd accepted a trial of some sort would be held before they moved on; that Jackson Farraday's guilt would be established in their minds, if only quasi-lawfully, and they could execute him with clear consciences.

Jackson's weapons and horses had been confiscated and he was under armed guard, but anyone was permitted to speak with him, though none did except Lil.

Jackson was unable to reassure her.

'Oh, they'll hang me all right, if Reiner is allowed to work on it and Petrie and Hannigan are prepared to turn a blind eye.'

'Maybe I could help you make a break for it. I could give you a gun, and none of them can shoot straight as me.'

'I don't think so, Lil. I've no mount and we can't fight the whole wagon train. They'd be on to the pair of us like a pack of wolves.'

Lil flung up her hands in frustration. 'We can't just sit here and do nothing!'

'We can't run either. We wouldn't stand a chance . . . it'd be ten to one against us getting away.'

'But the chances are a hundred to one against getting you out of this mess if we don't do something!' Lil retorted.

Silence descended on the pair as each digested the facts of the predicament.

Eventually, Jackson cleared his throat. 'What we have to do is undermine Reiner's case. In point of fact, it's flimsy enough anyway. I figure he's blackening me to settle my hash and hide a heap of secrets of his own.'

'Of course he is!' Lil cried in exasperation. 'It was him! He never went to Buzzard City. He just led you a dance — slugged you — killed Honesty — framed you.'

'Then maybe you'll agree. Instead of going off half-cocked, trying something rash and stupid, what you have to do is ride to Buzzard City now — today. It's no big place. Find a believable witness who can swear no stranger such as Reiner was in the Buzzard City saloon last night. The barkeep maybe. If he can write, get him to sign paper to that effect. Better yet, persuade the man to come back with you, or get whatever duly appointed peace officer they might have in town to witness his statement. Testimony that shows Reiner a liar will undermine the rest of his posturings.'

Lil silently acknowledged her mentor was right. If any law ruled in this section, it must have a duty to stop an unsanctioned hanging. She saw a slim chance that saner, more independent counsel than Winton Petrie's and the Reverend Hannigan's might yet be brought to bear.

'It's a long shot, but I'm damn sure you're right,' she said. 'Reiner never went where he said he did. Expose him over that and maybe the fools will also be able to accept you have no complicity in Honesty's odd death. I wonder if it can be done in time . . . '

Jackson grimaced, but tried to make it look ironic.

'If you don't get back, I'll be no worse off than I am now. Anyhow, to speak plain, I fear if you stay here you'll end up making trouble for the two of us.'

'No fooling! Hell, why didn't I think of all this? I should be halfway to Buzzard City already. I'm out of here!'

★ ★ ★

When Lilian Goodnight had left, Jackson Farraday felt twinges of misgiving. Had he done the right thing in sending her to Buzzard City? It was a wild and woolly town with an unsavoury reputation. Maybe he'd had no right to suggest a girl should ride there unaccompanied. But Lil was his only hope, the only person in the camp who believed in him. His situation was desperate.

And he'd given her something to do, which he realized was important in the circumstances. Because of the absurd and impractical regard she had for him, she wouldn't have stood by idly to watch him hanged.

Moreover, Lil had proved on many past occasions that she was uncommonly good at looking out for herself in dangerous places. He knew of no man who could better her prowess with a six-gun. In the Silver Vein country they called her the Princess of Pistoleers as well as Misfit. It wasn't for nothing.

Jackson began to feel a little better about what he'd done, but it didn't last many moments.

He noticed Luke Reiner was an interested spectator when Lil saddled up and rode out; also, that less than a minute later Reiner made his own hurried departure on horseback, as though he might be in pursuit.

Jackson started worrying again.

* * *

Lil had much on her mind. Her eyes were on the ribbon of trail to Buzzard

City as it descended, switching back on itself, into the gorge where the township's dwellings and primitive commercial buildings stood at odd angles like a herd of mangy old cows, dead or dying, stuck in a cold, mist-shrouded bog.

She didn't think to look back; she looked only ahead. She pushed Rebel unrelentingly through the softer, viscid footing of lower elevations where lately melted snow had yet to feel the drying warmth of a spring sun.

With a sense of small triumph, Lil had remembered she had in her possession the locket discarded by Honesty Petrie and containing the photographic portrait of Luke Reiner. It was a good likeness. Asking around and confirming suspicion that Reiner hadn't been in Buzzard City might be an easier job than it had first sounded. The blacks, browns, greys and dark greens of a soggy landscape were uniformly totally cheerless, but the picture — or rather thought of the assistance it would lend — was a boost to her spirits.

Just as she was moving into a mood of self-congratulation, any smugness was knocked right out of her. The vicious roar of a long gun set up shattering echoes in the upper reaches of the gorge.

'What the flaming hell — !'

The snarling whine of a big-calibre slug passed the back of her head. Lil twisted the reins round the pommel and dived from the saddle in a twisting ball of motion. She'd no time to pull her own rifle from its scabbard, but as she smacked into the soft ground, a Colt revolver left its holster and filled her right hand.

Her intelligent mount broke into a gallop, carrying on riderless down the trail, out of range and into safety.

Above Lil was a section of trail she'd already passed over, obscured in part by a clump of several varieties of timber, including thick-trunked Douglas fir and spruce. She figured it was from there the would-be dry-gulcher had chosen to mount his attack. It was a vantage point that both offered concealment and overlooked the next wind of the trail ahead.

It also occurred to her it was someone who'd probably followed her from the wagon camp. Reiner?

Crouching low, she hunted trailside cover in the form of a boulder — not ideal, not big, but big enough.

She was only a split-second in time. The rifle's angry roar blasted the silence again. Lil heard and felt the *plunk* of a bullet that buried itself in soft ground a scant foot from where she'd landed from the saddle.

Lil debated rushing on and regaining her horse before a third and maybe luckier potshot was fired at her. But there was no sense in that, she decided. Buzzard City was still a way off. No telling there was any certainty she'd be allowed to continue her journey. The dry-gulcher might know of other handy shooting nests downtrail.

Read the situation however you liked, fearlessly or fearfully she had to carry the fight to her unseen enemy while he was still cursing his failure to have cut her down in cold blood with his first or second shots.

Mud- and dirt-smeared from her fall, Lil zig-zagged upslope, taking her chances. Her objective was the trees that hid the rifleman at the crest of the rise.

The unknown fired another hurried shot.

It was of little account to Lil. She knew rifle shots at fast-moving people a tolerable distance away were seldom effective. Moreover, the front sight of the popular Winchester repeaters and other carbines would about cover a body. Even a good rifleman wasn't guaranteed where, or whether, his shot would hit an intended target.

The latest bullet sent her way succeeded in producing a groove in the rock to Lil's right, showering dust and chips, but it did no damage to her hide.

Getting into closer range, the time had come to do some shooting of her own. Though she couldn't hope with a belt-gun to nail this bastard just yet, she had to un-nerve him some!

Lil raised her Colt. She snapped off a couple of rapid shots. A highly skilled revolver shot with a well-kept weapon, she could hit a man at a range of fifty yards under favourable conditions. But she had precarious footing on a steep slope and entertained no such extravagant hopes. Her aim was to flush out her opponent. Her hard grey gaze raked the trees, but she saw no movement.

'Show yourself, mister, and you'll be almighty sorry, mark my words!' she yelled.

Smoking .45 at the ready in her fist, she darted from boulder to boulder. She swiftly drew near to the sniper's hiding place, but still no one showed himself.

The fast, uphill run and her wild challenge had left her breathless. She was reasonably sure her man had decamped. A last, lunging sprint from one piece of cover to another brought Lil almost to the big trees he'd used to hide behind. But before she could reach them, the sound of drumming hoofs came from the other side of the timbered ridge.

The dry-gulcher was maybe alarmed by Lil's plucky willingness to carry a fight to him, if not aware of her crackshot skill with a sixgun. Anyway, he hadn't waited to try conclusions with her. When she gained the crest, she saw her attacker had already retreated down the other side and was well away.

He had mounted his waiting horse and was disappearing at a creditable pace into a yonder that was the semi-desert habitat for an extensive stand of masking blackbrush. Some of the yellow-flowered, grey-green shrubs were fully fifteen feet high with numerous thorny branches.

The glimpses she caught of the incompetent and fleeing marksman, threading his way through the thickets, were insufficient to tell her with any certainty that he was Luke Reiner, though she had a gut feeling he could be no other.

Winded from scaling the steep slope and without a horse of her own readily to hand, she couldn't hope to chase him through the blackbrush on her own and catch him. Chance was that's what he figured she'd be foolhardy enough to try, and he'd wait someplace in ambush.

Disappointed at not having been able to shoot it out, Lil returned to the trail to locate Rebel . . . and to hope her vital mission to Buzzard City would suffer no more interruption.

9

Triumph and Failure

Though Jackson Farraday had not been entirely certain, Lil was convinced in her own mind that Luke Reiner was deeply implicated in the murder of Honesty Petrie. As Lil saw it, when Reiner's attempt to pass off the death as an apparent drowning had failed, he'd switched to an altogether more fiendish scheme that would both clear him of the crime and rid him of the scout he thought of as his rival.

Honesty had been winsomely pretty — most taking with her pigtails and sparkly blue eyes — and she'd been understandable to Lil, despite an irritating, silly way with men in their prime: men with whom she should have known better than to have toyed. Lil wanted to see her wasteful killing avenged. She also knew just how absurd was the wagoners' conviction that her murderer had been Jackson.

Jackson would never have taken, or allowed, liberties between himself and a girl so young. How many times had she herself wished Jackson would relax his rigid stance in this regard?

God, how she loved him! The times she'd prayed he would pay her the attentions she longed for! While he lived, she could hope and dream . . . and at the very least continue counting him as a reliable friend. How dire her situation would become if he was disgraced and hanged!

She was desperately anxious her visit to the notorious hell-hole called Buzzard City would not be in vain.

The township was no more attractive at close quarters than it had been at a distance; a sad tintype out of yesteryear recording the vestiges of a bygone boom. Its backdrop was the mini-mountains of tailings from the worked-out mines on which coarse weeds were struggling to establish a hold.

Lil rode down a winding grade that straightened out and became a pot-holed main street. She passed vacant lots and abandoned, tumbledown structures. The weight of the past winter's heavy snows had caused some roofs to collapse. Where the window glass hadn't been removed or smashed, and the windows boarded up, she peered through grimy panes into cobwebbed interiors, imagining the echoes of past business and life; of the quarrels, the feuds and the brawls; of the rash liaisons that were part and parcel of behaviour in undisciplined frontier towns.

She came to a saloon where a weather-cracked, faded board, a portion of which had fallen off, described the premises as the 'old Pot'. It was the only saloon still operating in Buzzard City. Although the hour was early for refreshment and recreation, it was open.

Lil dismounted and hitched Rebel to

the twisted rail out front. Through the creaking batwings, the atmosphere was as damp and dismal as outside. A few customers were huddled around one of the far tables but no one was at the slop-stained counter apart from the barkeep on the other side.

Lil fished out money and counted it — enough to buy whatever passed for a couple of glasses of whatever would pass here for whiskey. She spun a coin idly, nodded to the barkeep, slapped her money down and placed her request.

The fellow just gaped. 'Yuh're a lady,' he said as it dawned on him the buckskinned dude who'd just sauntered in and leaned an elbow on the bar wasn't a man.

'Well, female sure,' Lil conceded amiably.

'Don't serve no hard likker to unpart-nered wimmin — that is, wimmin without no men.'

'Why not?'

'They make trouble or get inta trouble. Makes no diffrence which. They'se trouble.

Git outa here, gal! Ain't safe fer unattached fillies in Buzzard City.'

'I know how to look after myself, and I'm not looking for trouble, I'm looking for a man.'

The barkeep whacked a damp cloth on the edge of his counter.

''Xactly! An' it'll lead to a fight.'

Then a shrewd thought struck him, visibly, and he said slyly, 'Though o' course, if a straight-limbed, clean-bodied gal were tough as she sounded, an' cared to prettify herself, lookin' to set up hereabouts in a line o' business, mebbe I c'd lend a hand . . . '

Lil kept her cool. 'You misunderstand me, mister. When I said I'm looking for a man, I meant a particular man.'

She produced Honesty's thrown-out locket and snapped it open to show the picture of Luke Reiner.

'This man! Have you seen him — say, just yesterday?'

'What's his name?'

'Luke Reiner, for what it's worth. Do you know him or not?'

'Never seen 'im. Not in the last day. Prob'ly never, though a tolerable number o' drifters passes through the mountains.' He looked her up and down. 'Done yuh wrong, has he?'

'Sort of.'

'Waal, yuh don't show yet so I'd advise yuh t' git rid of it. I don't know 'im an' can't give no help. Yuh'd better quit the saloon, pronto.'

Lil said, realizing he was a mite misled but knowing he'd said nothing she could agree to, 'No and no! I need you to swear this man hasn't been seen in the saloon. Make a statement under oath.'

'Uh . . . ?'

She figured it would be impossible for her to persuade the barkeep to desert the miserable saloon, which he probably owned as well as ran.

'Do you have a judge or an attorney in Buzzard City?'

The saloonman's expression switched from bewilderment to amusement. He laughed.

'Hell, gal, that's rich! We ain't even got no peace officer — no sheriff, no marshal, no constable, no jail. An' mebbe folks aim to keep it thataway.'

One of the men from the table in the corner sidled up to the bar. Lil's exchange with the apron had plainly caught his attention.

Lil didn't like the bunch's look. The four of them were rough, owlhoot types. The Henry Mountains were a hop, skip and jump west of the legendary Outlaw Trail that wound south from the Montana border, across Wyoming and through Utah on its way eventually to Old Mexico. Along the trail, men on the dodge were apt to hole up in fortress-like hideouts and law-abandoned towns like Buzzard City.

Much killing and robbing and raping took place in this man's country. Lil was confident of holding her own with the riff-raff one on one, but she didn't fancy her chances against a gang.

She quickly closed and palmed Honesty's locket and chain and slipped them back into her pocket. But she wasn't quick enough.

The man who'd come to the bar was lean and hard-faced with stubble on a jaw and cheeks that barely deserved the description clean-shaven. His clothes were worn range garb, but the two guns at his hips were well cared for. He looked born mean. And he was sharp-eyed, big-eared.

'Lookin' for someone, kid? You showin' a pi'cher?'

He was trying to assess her, and she knew he was puzzled. But she was making her own assessment — which was that all he and his down-and-out pards were looking for was a chance to cut themselves into some gravy that wasn't theirs. It might be no more than a silver locket and chain, but she had a hunch it might be more. She was an outnumbered, and therefore available, young woman in a place where a fresh body was scarce and had value.

He took her hesitation for fear, which

it half was. He produced a snaggle-toothed smile.

'I'm Clyde McCann. Me an' my brother Deke, we know most ever'body in this neck of the woods. Mebbe we know somethin' 'bout your feller.'

Lil swallowed. 'No. No, I don't think so. That's not exactly what I want.'

To tell these men she wanted them to front up to give evidence to a court — even a vigilante affair such as a party of emigrants planned to hold — wasn't on. Generally, hunted men wanted no contact with outsiders, known or unknown. Nor with law, official or unofficial. As for telling her whole story, that would summon no sympathy, for herself or a brave man who had scouted for the Army. She didn't think Clyde McCann, his brother and their two almost brutish associates were liable to be in any wise big-hearted.

'No,' she repeated. 'It was a mistake. I'd best be riding out.'

She'd scored a small triumph in establishing that Reiner had lied about spending his hours of absence visiting the saloon in Buzzard City. But it had immediately become a bitter thing, because she saw no clear way to capitalize on it.

In fact, she was up to her ears in trouble. She had to think fast to get herself out of it.

If she could report the finding to the wagoners, a slim chance existed some decent persons among them would check it out for themselves. If she swore to God her report was true — and why shouldn't it be? — perhaps they'd reconsider the harebrained proposal to put on trial and to hang an innocent man.

So Lil spun on a booted heel and ran for the batwings. She never reached them. The man who had to be Clyde McCann's brother Deke — he had the same close-set eyes — cut her off. She tried to dodge him, but he promptly thrust out a foot and a pushing, horny hand.

Lil crashed to the sawdust and the

dirt that covered the floor. It was ungallant, but really no surprise. Lil knew her world. She'd never had the delusion that every Western man was a New World version of the knight in shining armour. Many didn't tip their hats to all the ladies, be they honest women or whores or something in between. That was just a windy for the dime novelists.

Clyde laughed shortly. 'Look where you're goin', gal! You just done tripped over Deke's big clumsy foot!'

They hauled her to her feet, ostensibly brushing her off with hands that also felt and squeezed.

'She's a tastier dish than she's dressed!' one of the McCanns' friends said.

'No nevermind the duds. A change is gonna come — or mebbe no 'change' at all when we git her to the Hole an' help her outa 'em!'

Lil said in an earthy imperative and second-person pronoun what should be done to them, and managed to kick one in the shins.

'Owwww!'

But Clyde's right hand found its way into her coat pocket. It delved and pulled out Honesty's locket.

Leaving his sidekicks to restrain Lil, furious and struggling, Clyde opened up the hinged gew-gaw.

'Bull's-eye!' he said. 'It *is* him — Mark Steiner!'

Deke said heavily, 'Thought it might be.' He craned his neck to look at the picture. 'A mite older, but him anyways.'

Clyde demanded, 'Tell us, bitch — where is he?'

Lil said, 'Don't know, lunkhead! I was looking for him, wasn't I? And his name's Luke Reiner.'

Deke shrugged. 'Steiner — Reiner . . . it's him! And we ain't sure you was looking for him.'

Clyde's face came close to Lil's, teeth gritting. 'You ain't tellin' us all we want to know, but you will when we get you to the Hole.'

'What Hole are you talking about?'

she asked, though she had a notion.

White's Hole — originally White's Hidey-hole — was an infamous refuge in the vicinity for outlaws and nomadic gangs, based around a former ranch situated in an isolated valley where law-abiding settlers had long been content to leave society's misbegotten scum to their own devices.

Lil's heart sank when Clyde confirmed it. 'White's Hole.'

'I can tell you nothing; I don't want to go there!' she protested. 'It's a desolate, useless place.'

Deke leered. 'But plenty private. All birds go to singin' real nice at the Hole. We'll l'arn you likewise!'

One of his vulgar companions pinched her. She squeaked and managed to jerk an arm free. Her hand delivered a crisp slap to the offender's bristly face.

Deke roared with laughter.

The act of retaliation was futile, of course. The bunch took firm grip of her arms and marched her to the doors.

'Barkeep!' Lil cried. 'Tell these galoots to unhand me! Help! Get help!'

But the saloonman, whey-faced, had turned away and was minding his own business. He vigorously polished a glass with a grubby towel as though nothing at all was happening to claim his interest.

Screeching imprecations, Lil was dragged out of the Gold Pot like an obstreperous drunk. To her mortification and discomfort, they bound her wrist and ankle and threw her ignominiously across her saddle.

'Bastards!' she raged. 'There's no call to treat an inoffensive pilgrim this way!'

A big, hard hand was clapped over her mouth, silencing her.

'Shuddup! Or we'll stuff a balled kerchief in your mouth.'

She shut up.

Far worse than facing a journey to an unknown fate, head and feet down over Rebel's sides, was the knowledge she was failing Jackson Farraday.

And she was his last hope.

10

Turncoat Bandit

When it came to hell-holes, White's Hole beat Buzzard City hands down. The broad sweep of the outlaws' valley was dotted with soddies, dug-outs and cabins filthy and ramshackle beyond description. The land was for the most part poor graze. The enclosing, pinkish rock faces supported only straggly green cedars.

Here, as an uninformed, unwarned traveller, you'd be stumbling into the haunt of rustlers, road agents, bank robbers, train robbers. You'd be at the mercy of human vermin. Anyone who'd made his abode within the Hole's boundaries could be a murderer, or capable of it.

At the very best, the McCanns' bunch meant to throw a scare into her,

Misfit Lil thought. At the Hole, they could do what they liked with impunity.

They untied her ankles and took her from her horse and into a weather-beaten but sturdy barn behind a cabin off the valley road. She was shaken and sore in strange places from the ride. As the door swung open and light shafted in, a big brown rat scuttled across the floor and scampered up the side of a rotting wagon that occupied one corner pursuing the silent, slow progression into disintegration.

The barn was a place of mouldering hay and rotting harness. It had a smell compounded of decay, old horse piss and dung, and human sweat.

'She's got a poor memory, or she's lying,' Clyde told the others. 'I figure she knows where Steiner is. String her up from the beam.'

'You can't do this!' Lil blurted.

Clyde grinned repellently. 'We do what we want in our own place.'

A rope was threaded under the tight bonds at her wrists and thrown up into the gloom under the rafters above. They hauled on the returning end, jerking her arms up over her head and stretching her slim body so her toes were just touching the ground. She gave only one sharp cry.

'Get a whip, Yancey!' Clyde said. 'We'll thrash the truth outa her. A few stripes and bruises an' she'll talk.'

It was no bluff and Deke winked evilly. 'After it's done, she'll be fit to refuse us *nothin'*, boys.'

'Don't we take them buckskins off first?' Yancey said.

Yancey was prematurely bald in a time when a shiny dome was not deemed an admirable fashion. These were four tough and wild men, and Yancey was the meanest, the most ornery.

Lil suppressed a shiver. The mark of dissoluteness was on them all and at the Hole there'd be more of their ilk in close proximity — heartless, brutal, lusting for fresh objects for their cruel sport. They'd relish the chance to torment her in the most terrible ways imaginable.

Lil had once seen a girl who'd been whipped. Bits of tattered clothes had had to be soaked from her slashed and bloodied back. She'd suffered agony.

The only course open was to cut a deal, Lil decided.

'All right, fellers!' she conceded quickly. 'There's no need for any of this. I'm ready to throw in and play your game. Let me down and I'll be a good girl. I've no love for Reiner anyhow. You tell me what he's done to you and I'll tell where he is.'

Clyde jeered, 'What price loyalty now, huh? Well, the double-crossin' louse don't deserve better.'

Lil didn't even try to disabuse him of the notion she was shielding Reiner.

'What did he do?'

Clyde thought about it.

'Mebbe you did oughta know what your two-timin' man is apt to do with folks he no longer can use . . . '

'He isn't mine. Cut me down and tell me!'

Clyde sniggered. 'By what right d' you give any orders?'

'None. But I'm going to lead you to Reiner, aren't I?'

Clyde allowed himself a self-satisfied smile and made a gesture. He was happy enough his strategy had worked and his brother and the boys could see he had everything under his smart control. Lil was lowered — though a mite reluctantly and roughly, she felt.

Clyde talked.

'Steiner rode with my bunch way back before Buzzard City's mines were played out. We snatched a cheatin', greedy minin' outfit's ten-thousand-dollar payroll from the Overland stage. The robbery didn't go as planned 'cause a posse of detectives was ridin' shotgun inside the coach. In the skirmish, we lost sight of Steiner. He rode out on the gang, but his mask slipped as he made his getaway an' he was recognized by a Pinkerton. He was later arrested in Colorado and sent to serve time in the territorial penitentiary.'

'So . . . ' Lil said, puzzled. 'You got away free, didn't you?'

'Yeah, but Steiner took the payroll that was s'posed to've been split between us. It wasn't recovered by the lawdogs. He must've stashed the haul someplace close, intending to come back later an' collect it for hisself alone. Me an' my brother've scoured the countryside since an' never found it.'

Deke got impatient. He cut in accusingly, 'You been hobnobbin' with him, bitch, ain't you? Steiner always had a hankerin' for sassy young women, though I figured he preferred 'em kinda more doll-like. Used to keep 'em on a string till he'd gotten 'em mussed up perm'nent, kinda spoiled inside an' out, so's their mamas an' papas wouldn't know 'em!'

But Clyde saw no point in emphasizing these angles of the situation.

'The turncoat's back, ain't he?' he

demanded of Lil. 'An' not past female-botherin' years, I guess. Where did you lose him? He picked up the payroll dinero an' dumped you, didn't he?'

'Our day has come!' Deke said. 'We want our share of the money an' more. Jest tell us where he left you.'

Lil was thinking fast. She reckoned the day might have come, too. All manner of pieces were falling into place. She knew at last why Luke Reiner — or Mark Steiner — had brought the wagon train on the little-used route to the south. The long-hidden stolen money explained the mysterious 'fortune' Reiner had claimed was waiting for him with a 'cousin in California'. On the night before Honesty's murder, when Reiner was followed by Jackson Farraday, he'd likely been going to recover it. Maybe he had it with him now, in his packs at the wagon train's camp.

'Get your mouth movin', kid!' Deke said. ''Cause Clyde's told you stuff don't mean you're outa the woods yet.'

Yancey gripped her by the hair and thrust his face up to hers.

'Talk!' he rasped. And she got a faceful of spit and foul breath tinged with sour, rotgut whiskey.

Lil put her cards on the table.

'It's true! Reiner is all you say and worse. He's trying to frame an innocent man for the murder of Honesty Petrie, a wagon captain's sweet and only daughter who was grown-up too early for her years and good sense.'

Once Lil started to tell her story, it was as though she couldn't stop. At the back of her mind was an alluring notion that she could strike a bargain with the McCanns: help them claim 'their' money if they'd swear to the fact that Luke Reiner had not been in the saloon at Buzzard City when he said he was, on the night that Honesty was murdered and her body thrown in the creek to make it look like a drowning.

'Reiner is making a poor fist of pretending to be a wagon train scout,' she poured out. 'I'll take you to where the wagon train is camped, along the road apiece north of Buzzard City. Reiner must've killed Honesty because she rejected him, having a none-too-secret longing for this other, much finer man: my friend Jackson Farraday. Maybe she tipped Reiner over the edge by telling him she put what she kidded herself was true love before all that money he'd promised to bring her.'

But the McCanns were unmoved by the complexities of her report. They listened with sneering malice.

Lil pressed on. 'Maybe Reiner is — '

'Yeah, all of what you're saying is no more'n as *maybe*,' Clyde said, speaking up over her. 'We don't need a bar of such a mess of trouble! A wagon train. That won't be hard to pick out on the Buzzard City road. We'll find it our ownselves.'

'What do you mean? I'm coming along. I've got to get back.'

'We don't need no guide. You still look like mischief to me an' you stay here. If your story's moonshine — if'n we don't get Steiner an' the money — you pay plenty when we get back. Unnerstand?'

Lil's rising spirits did an about-turn and some sinking.

Then Yancey put in his two bits' worth.

'There could be other pickin's in this. A wagon train packed full o' sodbusters' worldly wealth. Don't see much o' sich hereabouts no more.'

His companion, the fourth man, nodded a squarish head and flexed big-jointed fingers.

'That's right. Mebbe we should get together a big gang of the Hole crowd and get our hands on the whole kit an' boilin'. Those Eastern greenhorns won't have a prayer.'

Clyde said, 'Smart thinkin', Arch! We'll do it. It's a stroke of luck. An extra we could use. Who the hell's to stop us?'

His brother was in enthusiastic agreement.

'Nobody, Clyde. Wagon trains get wiped out in floods, burned by Indians . . . it'd cause nary a flutter if this 'un never turned up again. A disaster someplace, they'd say. No evidence left to prove nothin'. Meanwhile, with all the loot to be had, we'd be the toast of the Hole.'

Lil's blood ran cold. The outlaws were planning a massacre, and her stupidity, or her desperation to avoid a whipping and worse, would be the cause of it!

Now, not only Jackson's life was in the balance, but a whole community of men, women and children.

'I won't stay here by myself!' Lil said.

Clyde was amused by her adamancy.

'Oh, you won't be left by yourself. You'll have comp'ny. Broken-Nose Ginny lives in the house with Deke an' me. She'll look after a young friend for us real well . . . '

All four of the men laughed as though this was a huge joke.

'Come an' meet Ginny!' Deke said.

He grabbed her tied wrists and dragged her after him.

'Who's Ginny?' Lil demanded. 'Is she another poor girl you've tricked?'

Clyde enjoyed giving her an answer.

'Ginny's a consumptive whore we brung from Denver to keep house an' like. Is that any crime? Hell, she knows it was a kindness. It was for her health, an' her looks was about gone. Paint an' the dark could scarce hide it.'

They all trooped across a wide verandah into the ramshackle, one-storey cabin, which was a much bigger erection than it had looked from the road. Inside, everything was filthy. It was a bastion of male slovenliness that Ginny had been unable, unwilling, or plain forbidden to change.

The rugs were matted with dirt, the furniture was thick with dust that had become grime on handled surfaces. Months of grey ashes clogged the fireplace and sifted on to an unscrubbed, unpolished floor of uneven and creaking boards. The vestiges of past meals in the form of food scraps and unwashed dishes had been left adorned with mangled cigarette ends on a stained, knotty pine table that stood lopsided on its uneven legs.

Flies buzzed and crawled.

Lil, always most at home in the clean, open air, felt her stomach churn in repugnance.

Broken-Nose Ginny herself was a tragic figure of a kind not unknown to Lil. Her age was hard to determine. Maybe before her nose had got broken and disease had taken its toll she'd had a fine-featured, wide-eyed beauty. But fate had shown her too much sleaziness and misery too quickly, fading her charms early. Now, the eyes were big and dark only with the despair of apprehension about the men she served.

She held herself stiff and attentive, like a frequently chastised child. Most of the men in White's Hole would be barbarians where women were concerned. Having never known how to look out for herself, Ginny likely led a wretched life here.

'Who's she?' she asked, fixing on Lil with her stare.

'Call the bitch a friend of a friend,' Deke said. 'It's your job to see she stays nice an' safe. We got business to see to. We're goin' a-ridin' an' she better be here when we get back.'

'All right, but what if she wants to quit?'

'She don't. You don't let her.'

'She got guns.'

Arch said, 'But her hands are tied.'

Clyde said, 'First thing you can do, Ginny, is take off her belt and holsters an' the guns. It'll make us all feel easier.'

Lil didn't resist when Ginny approached to carry out the order. It would have been pointless.

At close quarters, Ginny smelled of lavender water masking an odour that suggested she should wash more often. Either she didn't notice it herself or she'd lost all pride. Her hair was bunched in a knot on the top and back of her head, but strands had escaped, straggly and greasy. Her face was white and pinched.

Ginny said dully, 'What's your name, girl?'

'Lil.'

Ginny said abruptly to her bosses, 'I don't trust her. She's young and strong. I don't want her in here. Why's she wearing men's garb? Why's she heeled anyhow? Bound wrists and hands won't fix much if she wants to light out.'

Clyde said, 'No, but you'll fix it, Ginny, or else . . . '

Yancey said, 'We don't want to lose her, slut.'

Deke had the solution. 'We'll take her back to the barn an' put the bar across the door outside. That way it'll be right easy for you, Ginny.'

Alarm leaped in Ginny's eyes. She swallowed.

'The rats . . . '

Lil picked up fast. 'Hell, yeah, the barn is crawling with the brazen varmints! I saw one — heard 'em.'

If she wasn't overly frightened of a rat or two, Ginny, she figured, was. And Lil was planning ahead. If she was going to get out of this tight, she'd need to. Playing on whatever fears Ginny had would be no bad move.

'Too bad,' Deke said. 'We'll be back inside of a day, mebbe two. The rats won't have gnawed away too much of your beauty!'

He laughed hugely at his own joke and the other men chortled. Ginny, Lil noted, shivered although the room, occupied by four sweaty male bodies plus herself and Ginny, was close and warm.

To Lil, it seemed the most pressing need was for her to return to the wagon train and be of help to it and Jackson before a gang from White's Hole, led by the McCanns, could complete a vicious raid. Reiner, or Steiner, and his past movements were now the least of her problems.

Something in her devious mind

produced the hunch that she'd have a better chance of achieving her objective if she was incarcerated in the rat-infested barn rather than held under thin-faced Ginny's watchful, dark eyes in the smelly cabin.

She maintained her protest, appealing to the other men.

'Arch, Yancey, you wouldn't put a poor girl in with the rats, would you? I hate the sneaking critters! Wherever you see one, there's sure to be hundreds. Their filthy coats and trailing tails are full of fleas and all kinds of death-dealing germs and ills: the fever, diarrhoea, cholera, the typhus! You wouldn't want me if I had anything like that, would you?'

Clyde was dismissive.

'Aw, they'll be scared o' you first day or two an' we won't be gone no longer'n that. Ransackin' a wagon train'll take no time at all. Pickin' off them clodhoppers'll be like shootin' fish in a barrel. Anyways, the rats are just pack rats, woman. Wood rats.'

Lil didn't know that was true. The wood rats of the desert country built their nests outdoors and were primarily nocturnal and vegetarian, often finding their water in succulent plants. They survived on a diet of spiny cactus, yucca pods, bark, berries, piñon nuts, seeds and any available green vegetation. Moreover, Lil didn't want any of them, especially her prospective jailer Ginny, to think these could be the less forbidding pack rats.

'The one I saw was a brown rat — dirtier, bigger, hairy-tailed,' she insisted. 'Didn't you know? They're tougher and more adaptable to conditions. They're ousting the pack rats in places like this, settling in and breeding by the hundreds. One day it'll be rats against people. They'll be under the floors, in the roofs . . . '

Ginny shuddered and suppressed a moan.

'Shuddup!' Deke barked. 'You damn well will go in the barn, bitch, that's final!'

She was hauled back forcibly to the dim, even more malodorous barn.

'This stinks every which way, Mister Clyde McCann! Hell, we made a deal and you're not playing square. Jackson Farraday is going to be hanged by your clodhoppers, because Reiner has bamboozled them.'

Clyde's face kept its unsympathetic sneer.

'If'n we're there in time after we've gotten the raidin' party together, this Farraday fool'll get a fair shake, long as he don't stand in our way.'

'How will he know he's standing in the way of his rescuers if they're attacking the wagon train?'

Clyde scorned her plea with sarcasm.

'He'll see it on our friendly mugs! Ginny, tell 'er how we treat folks that don't co-operate.'

Ginny said her piece dispiritedly, but she was also a mite more frank than Lil had expected.

'You better shush, gal. The McCanns ain't never needed no more excuse than supper bein' late to the table, or a saying of the wrong word at the wrong moment, to beat up on anybody. Oft-times they'll make a lady wait on them with no clothes on, just because they're drunk, or on account of they need a bait of relief from their frustrations.'

Deke said, 'See? We always get what we want. An' remember this: you try so much as stickin' your beak outa this here barn afore we're back an' Ginny'll shoot you on the spot. She knows what'll happen to her if she don't obey orders.'

11

Prisoners' Woes

The passing of the sun across the sky and the failure of Lil Goodnight to return to the wagon camp was deeply disturbing to Jackson Farraday.

They'd shackled him to the big offside wheel of Winton Petrie's wagon. Jackson knew they were rustling up the collective courage to carry out Luke Reiner's urgings — to try him for the murder of Petrie's daughter and summarily to hang him.

But what had happened to Lil Goodnight? He felt responsible for her safety, though he was powerless to do a jot about it. From the get-go, it had been a long shot that Lil would secure evidence in Buzzard City that would cheat the wagoners' hangrope of his neck. He cursed himself for letting the girl go.

Catching sight of the Reverend James Hannigan, he hailed him.

Scowling, the dour preacher came over.

Jackson said, 'Miss Goodnight was going to Buzzard City to check out certain facts. She hasn't returned and I'm worried. Someone needs to go find what has happened to her.'

Hannigan shrugged the square shoulders of his black coat.

'I don't think so, Mr Farraday. A girl of that sort is likely to have taken up with some beguiling roughneck. She was never one of our party and has probably run off to start over someplace else. I hope so.'

'You're not over fond of Miss Goodnight or me, are you?'

'No, sir, I am not. I am out of temper with fondness. The law has been broken. Thou shall not kill . . . even when the victim was a girl who was not as good as she ought to have been.'

Hannigan's voice trembled. With conviction? Or with something else?

Jackson ignored what sounded like the presumption of his guilt. He was fast getting used to it. Not one of the wagoners would look him in the face or give him the time of day. But he was intrigued to know what the grim parson might tell about Honesty Petrie and her doings.

'What does that mean? What was it that was bad about Miss Petrie?'

Hannigan said gustily, 'Come now, you would not have me speak ill of the dead, but Miss Petrie was a well-known flibbertigibbet. She was leading my daughter Prudence astray. I will not say more.'

Jackson was in no position to coax or coerce. The likelihood was that the stony-faced proselytizer had viewed Honesty Petrie in the same light as he evidently saw Lil Goodnight: fond of fun and laughter and seducing his Prudence from the straight and narrow of strict religious beliefs. Hannigan had too much of the Puritan in him to approve of either Honesty or Lil.

Yet there was a strangeness about him, too, stranger than the partly understandable distaste occasioned by his devout calling and parental concern.

Jackson made one last attempt.

'I'd find it hard to live with myself, Reverend, if I were to allow another girl's life to end in evil circumstances.'

'I understand the girl is known as Misfit Lil, and a misfit is what she is. What that wild young woman has done — where she has gone — is outside my province.'

The words tumbled out of him and his Adam's apple bobbed like a juggler's ball trapped in the scrawny skin of his throat.

Frowning in puzzlement, Jackson took another line.

'Then you must speak in my behalf, so I can ride pronto to that province. How can you stand by and witness, if not advocate, the folly of my own lawless condemnation? And you a man of the cloth!'

Hannigan's eyes glinted like freshly

struck nailheads, but he didn't back down.

'You are treated well enough.'

'Sure. I'm being treated like a mad-dog killer might deserve, but I'm not a mad-dog killer.'

Hannigan didn't meet Jackson's eyes this time. He turned away evasively.

'I wouldn't know that for a fact.'

'Therefore you don't mind if I'm kept chained up and no attempt is mounted to check any other suspect — to expose whoever else might be Honesty Petrie's killer!'

Hannigan drew himself up to deliver his final denunciation, speaking as though by rote.

'Temporal law is not my responsibility. The will and the Word of God are paramount. The righteous and the good shall survive and prosper; the evil shall be punished and die. So it is written in the Book.'

He stalked away. Jackson, wrathful, was left to fret and to wonder in his chains.

Ever since her vexed father had sent her from the Flying G ranch to the high-toned academy in Boston to mend her tomboy ways, Misfit Lil had found confined spaces depressing. But the McCanns' barn made her feel worse than that. Gentle incarceration with the vapid, twittering daughters of Eastern gentlefolk — whom she'd proceeded to enlighten in the facts of real life — was nothing like cruel imprisonment in a stinking barn with sleek, disease-ridden rats for company.

Each and every one of the cogent arguments that she'd be a sight more use to the brothers riding along with the scratch gang they planned to raise to plunder Winton Petrie's wagon train had been rejected. She was left to seethe. Her only, untender care was to be provided by the unfortunate Broken-Nose Ginny.

As an extra precaution, the McCanns had taken her boots, leaving her barefooted to pace the dirty hay of her prison.

The horrific thought occurred to her that if she slept, the rats, who were constantly scuttling and scampering might come and gnaw at her toes. From the noise they made, dozens of them had to be nesting and breeding prolifically in the barn's mess.

On top of the physical discomfort was the mental torture of knowing that Jackson Farraday would not be relieved from his fate at the hands of Luke Reiner and the emigrants by the kind of intervention plotted by the McCanns. As their scout, her hero would consider it his responsibility and a point of honour to defend the inexperienced pioneers against any attack on the wagon train, no matter how badly he had been treated.

She feared Jackson was doomed, one way or another. Unless she could escape, quickly . . . only then might he have some small, dim chance of survival.

As soon as her eyes grew accustomed to the gloom, Lil began an inspection of her fetid surroundings. She didn't doubt that she could, in time, free her hands. Somewhere in the barn's clutter, or the wreck of the decaying wagon, she'd find some suitably sharp edge that she could use to saw through the tight ropes. But then what?

The walls of the barn were solid. Though a prolonged search might reveal the holes through which the rats made their entry or the occasional departure, she couldn't use rat holes herself without considerably enlarging them, which would be noted by Broken-Nose Ginny. It would, in any case, be far too long a job without decent tools.

It might take the McCanns a few hours to raise their gang, to ride out and find the wagon camp. But the clock she didn't have was ticking . . .

No; escape would have to be achieved near enough immediately. The only way out was through the barred door. The question was how.

In an untidy corner behind the wagon, she found inspiration. The discarded clutter presumably left by former ranching-family owners included a collection of glass preserving jars. Her scheme came in a flash, complete and surely perfect.

The jars would be the keys to her jail.

Such containers were familiar enough to Lil. Home food-preserving was part and parcel of her Western life. One of the greatest challenges armies had faced in the early nineteenth century was feeding troops. Through this, hermetic preserving of food had come about. The invention of the fruit jar — or Mason jar as it was later called — had made life easier for both rural and urban households after the time of the War Between the States. Best of all, midwinter meals had become more nutritional and palatable.

The revolutionary invention allowed families to prepare for a harsher and colder season by 'putting up' the fruits and vegetables they had in abundance in the fall. Along with pickling, drying and smoking, the process had become commonplace.

To a resourceful mind, like Lil's, preserving was a fascinating, practical subject in which she was well-versed.

She examined critically the trove of old and dusty jars and their lids.

Various designs were represented with patents dating from the middle of the century. Raised lettering on one jar said it was a 'MILLVILLE ATMO-SPHERIC FRUIT JAR'; several had a thumbscrew clamp and glass-lid design where the castmetal clamp held down a lid which fitted over a grooved mouth, or into the jar neck, which was fitted by the user with an indiarubber gasket to effect the seal.

Lil settled on the tallest and largest of the jars as the centrepiece of her ingenious escape plan.

The inscription on this one read 'MASON'S PATENT NOV 30TH 1858'. It had the familiar, simpler closure method of a thread moulded into its top and a zinc lid with a rubber ring to produce the seal between the lid and the jar.

All Lil knew about Mr John L. Mason, inventor of the jar, was that he'd been a tinsmith from New York City and he'd been aged 26 when he'd filed the patent for his now famous Mason jar. It amused her to wonder what this young man had been like, and what he would have said about the use to which she proposed to put his contribution to the history and health of the American nation.

'Well,' she murmured, 'I guess you could say it could prove just as lifegiving as any preserving session!'

But first she had to get her bait . . .

Lil started hollering.

'*Ginny! Ginny!*'

She repeated the call over and over at the top of her lungs and rattled the barn doors.

Predictably, the slatternly young woman rushed from the house.

'What is it? I vow and declare I never heard such carrying-on!'

'I'm hungry,' Lil said through the barred door.

'What of it? You won't die. The McCanns didn't say I was to feed you.'

'They didn't say you wasn't either, did they? Suppose when they come back I'm faint from lack of nourishment? They won't be pleased, will they? I think you should bring me grub!'

'It's a trick. I open the doors with the grub and you'll run out and get away.'

'No I won't.'

'Yes you will. Then they'll do me instead. You don't know what they're like with a girl. They make a circle around you. They break open a keg of moonshine whiskey; make you swallow lots of the fiery stuff; get drunk theirselfs. Then they take turns at you, over and over and over till you're hurt real bad inside.'

'Look, if I don't eat, I'll faint away and they'll have you anyway, in my stead. I don't care if they do rape me,'

174

she lied, 'long as I've eaten before to keep up my strength.'

Ginny considered Lil's claims, but was dubious.

'You don't know what you're saying, and you don't sound weak from hunger.'

'I am! I'm dizzy with it. But all right, if that's what you want — let them find me passed out. You be their plaything. Sounds like it won't be a first time.'

After a long silence and some uncertain foot-shuffling, Ginny finally said, 'Oh, all right, I s'pose it won't do no harm . . . '

'Good.'

'But remember — when I open this door, the grub'll be set on the ground for dragging in and I'll be pointing a shotgun loaded with buckshot.'

Lil silently rejoiced. She'd never supposed Ginny would bring her food — and open the door — without taking a few obvious precautions.

Stage one of her scheme was complete. She hoped the remaining parts would be as successful.

12

The Way Out

Less than ten minutes elapsed before Ginny returned. Lil heard her fumbling with the heavy wooden beam that slotted into two iron brackets solidly bolted through the frame to hold shut the door.

Ginny the young-old whore was true to her word. When the door swung back, creaking, Lil found herself staring down the barrels of a shotgun — two dark, unwinking eyes that at such close quarters could belch a sudden death so bloody she'd be unrecognizable.

As she'd expected, she had no chance to break free. Yet.

At Ginny's feet was a bowl and a plate. The bowl contained what looked like stew and smelled more like warm ordure. The plate had on it a hunk of coarse bread and a piece of cheese speckled green and leprous white with patches of mould.

'It's all I can find to dare give you,' Ginny said. 'Pull it in and don't let me hear you shouting no more!'

Lil wrinkled her nose and took the disgusting food as bidden. She managed to say, 'Thank you,' though not especially meekly.

Ginny gave Lil's still tied wrists a glance, plainly found that reassuring, and departed. Lil heard her heave and wrestle the locking beam back into its brackets with a few testy grunts and a choice oath. Which left her to her own devices with the unappetizing booty.

Leastways, to Lil the offered meal was unappetizing. The stew was the sonofabitch variety — a concoction of heart, liver, testicles and other organs. No prime cuts had been wasted in its preparation. Its temperature was tepid only. Lil noted big, floating rings of fat were starting to congeal conveniently on its surface. The ripe cheese and the bread would doubtless serve for her purposes, too.

But first she had to turn her attention to freeing her restricted hands. She had greater ambitions than to feed herself. She took the most fragile-looking of the glass preserving jars and smashed it against the three-eights-inch-thick iron tyre that covered the rim of one of the wagon's wheels. Shards fell with a muffled tinkle to the hay-strewn floor.

She worked diligently to saw and fray at the ropes around her wrists, trying not to cut herself. Jagged glass and wrists were a frightening combination and she couldn't afford for this to go wrong. At last she snapped the remaining strands with a tug.

'Phew!' she gasped, glad that part was safely done.

She turned her attention to the tallest Mason jar, removing its screwtop lid and carrying it to the foul stew. Her nose twitched in revulsion as she scooped the globs of rancid fat off the murky brown surface. She rubbed the lumps with her fingers inside the neck of the jar. It made a slippery, smeary mess. As food, the meat fat would be the pits; as grease it would serve admirably.

Next came the cheese and the bread: the real bait.

She crumbled them, noting with satisfaction that the cheese was about the highest she'd smelled, ever. She tipped the crumbs into the jar. Most of them dropped to its bottom.

Lil wedged the jar upright between a shadowed, collapsed wheel and the body of the wagon. And she sat down to watch and wait. She nursed a desperate hope that expected developments did not take too much of the precious time she judged might be left for breaking out and carrying warning to the wagon train and Jackson Farraday of the threatened raid by the McCanns.

The rustlings of the rats that infested the barn had been constant. Predictably, the smells of food had not gone unnoticed by the vermin. Lil didn't reckon it was mere wishful thinking that the critters' furtive activity had stepped up a notch.

In no time at all, a dark shape emerged from a far corner and scuttled like a moving shadow across the floor to the wagon. It froze slyly beside the wheel.

Lil also kept perfectly still.

The rat was brown with a long, whiskered snout. It had a whitish underside and feet, small ears and a long hairy tail that made up fully a third of its twelve-inch length. Though not given to irrational fears herself, Lil did find something sinister — a suggestion of the primeval — about its silhouette and its movements or lack of them.

Rats had voracious appetites and intense curiosity. Lil knew this one, which had responded fastest to the lure of the strong-smelling food, would not delay too long, lest it find itself in competition with others of its colony.

Go on up and in, Mister Rat, Lil pleaded silently.

As though in answer to her will, the fat body and swishing tail glided up the spokes of the wagon wheel. The rat took a header into the waiting, open-topped jar with its overpowering scent of rich tidbits.

Lil rose and rushed forward, jar lid in hand.

The rat, sensing her approach, turned as swiftly as it could in the confines of the jar and tried to climb out. The clawed, pink forefeet were like four-fingered hands with long, pointed fingernails. They scrabbled at the fat-greased glass but couldn't gain sufficient purchase fast enough to effect an exit.

Lil clapped the lid over the aperture and twisted. She thought she heard the rat squeal. The foolhardy varmint was trapped, a victim of its omnivorous greed.

So far, so good, Lil thought. Now for stage three of the plan.

Other rats were already gathering boldly and unconcernedly, feasting from the abandoned bowl containing the remnants of ghastly stew. Lil ignored them. She started to scream.

'Help! Help! I'm bleeding to death! Save me, oh, save me!'

She repeated the cries, carrying on in a similar vein and making as big a racket as she could till Broken-Nose Ginny stomped up and rattled the door.

'Shut up, you bothersome brat!'

'But I'm dying. There were some old jars in here. I've stepped on broken glass in my bare feet. I'm cut awful bad! I'll die if I can't staunch the blood. Oh God, help me, Ginny . . . you must help me!'

'You silly bitch! I can't help you.'

Lil moaned despairingly. 'Bring me bandages, rags — anything to stop the bleeding!'

'That's enough! Be quiet, I say!'

'I soon will be — I'll be fainted clean away! What will the McCanns do then? They won't like it if I'm bled to death. They'll blame you prob'ly. They were going to have fun with me. Now they'll punish you something fierce! Oh! Oh! Oh!'

Ginny growled unintelligibly, then relented.

'All right. I'll bring you some towels and stuff. But I'll also be carrying the shotgun, mind. So no tricks, d'you hear?'

Ginny went away, still hostile but evidently successfully pushed into doing what Lil willed. She had the aura of a woman who'd spent her life being pushed around.

But Lil couldn't let sympathy divert her from her course.

Ginny quickly returned and Lil was ready when she lifted out the heavy timber that held the door solidly shut.

She stayed to one side of the opening door, clutching the Mason jar with its writhing contents, one hand ready to lift the unscrewed lid.

Ginny appeared with grubby towels and strips of torn cotton over her shoulder — and the shotgun in her hands.

Lil let the lid of the Mason jar fall and, holding the vessel in both hands, tossed its contents.

The rat hurtled out and landed on Ginny's top-knot of hair. The piled tresses promptly came loose and tumbled to her thin shoulders with the rat's prehensile limbs and tail grasping for holds.

Ginny yelped in terror.

One barrel of the shotgun went off with a roar. Pellets peppered the far wall of the barn and the wrecked wagon.

But Ginny dropped the fearsome weapon directly and shook her shabby black skirt, to which the falling rat was clinging as though for dear life.

Lil swooped on the gun before the echoes of its blast died. She cocked the left hammer. It made a loud, metallic double-click. She couldn't tell whether Ginny had heard it above the din of her own screaming panic.

'There's the other barrel left!' Lil yelled. 'Hadn't you best start worrying about that?'

The rat, which was as startled and frightened as Ginny, dropped to the ground and leaped back into the shadows of the barn, its long tail snaking behind it.

Ginny wailed as she realized Lil had tricked her, had come out of her prison and was very much in charge.

'No nonsense, Ginny,' Lil said. 'I want my boots, my guns and my horse. Else, you go in the barn with all the rats!'

She didn't feel proud of what she'd done and was doing to the McCanns' drudge; from her account, the woman was truly more sinned against than sinning. Living in White's Hole, Lord knew what she'd been through . . . well, the Devil anyway, Lil corrected herself.

'You fooled me, Lil — you lied about cutting your foot,' Ginny accused. 'It's mean what you did with the food I gave you, and the stuff you found in the barn. How did you get to be so sneaky?'

Lil shrugged.

'Ranch girls learn early in life how to

use all the material bits and pieces around. The tools you own might be few and therefore have many uses. In lean years, when the Flying G was struggling, I saw the hands make traps for rats with old bottles. They were very like the one I made with the Mason jar. Every container, every scrap of timber or metal, every bit of wire has a purpose. You and the McCanns should learn lessons like that before you sink to crime to make your way in life.'

The advice fell on deaf ears.

'Clyde, Deke and the others will kill me for letting you get loose!'

Lil said, 'They might not be back here for hours, Ginny, if ever. You'd do best to quit this place soon as you get the chance, if not now. Come on, take me to my stuff, and be quick about it.'

She prodded the unfortunate forward with the barrels of the shotgun.

Sometime, life might be made better, easier for Broken-Nose Ginny. Her hardships might be brought to an end and her health improve.

Lil hoped so, but she had to follow her own trail. With Jackson Farraday and the wagon train unknowingly dependent on her intervention to save them from a ruthless raid, none of it could be attended to today.

Lil wouldn't entertain notions of guilt about tricking Ginny and leaving her at White's Hole. The sickly prostitute had already had no future, only a past.

13

Cheating the Hangrope

Misfit Lil set out on Rebel from Buzzard City in a mile-eating lope. She'd ascertained from the reluctant barkeeper at the saloon that the outlaw McCanns hadn't left town more than two hours previous after recruiting a gang of roughnecks and hardcases.

Their tracks trended in the general direction of the Petrie wagon train, but it was clear Clyde McCann's confidence that his ransackers would locate it without Lil's guidance had been arrogant. They would lose many unnecessary hours scouring the breaks southeast of Buzzard City. The places for a rider to top out were few and the broken country did not lend itself to sweeping vistas of the terrain. A wagon train on the move or stationary could be easily hidden from view in any one of a number of canyons or passes.

The springtime sun dropping at her back, Lil abandoned following the bunch's tracks and headed directly for the place where she'd left the wagon camp early in the eventful day.

A full-scale meeting of the emigrants was in progress when Lil rode in. She dropped from her saddle and ran right into the middle of the solemn assembly, which was being addressed by Winton Petrie.

His subject was his daughter, Honesty, her accused murderer, the prisoner, Jackson Farraday, and what was to be done with him.

'We don't know this man as thoroughly as we might, though he has reputation and standing in the West. However, he has a case to answer and might be dangerous — '

'Bullshit!' Lil cried. 'Jackson is innocent. He'll do you no harm. Lies have been told, and I now can tell you some of them! But you talk of danger and there is one — an imminent danger of which you know nothing. You must stop this silly palaver right away and — '

Luke Reiner jumped to his feet, his face full of angry blood.

'The girl is in cahoots with Farraday! She's another he's despoiled, but this one's a whore and proud of it. Don't listen to a word of her drivel!'

The meeting exploded in uproar.

Reiner had to bawl to make the rest of his message heard. 'Don't let her make you feel sorry for the bastard — hang him right away!'

'Yeah, enough of the shilly-shallying,' a woman croaked harshly. 'Pretty Honesty weren't given no second chances. One of you big men, fetch a rope! Tie a noose! Let's see the fornicatin' child-killer dance on air an' empty hisself one last time — in his pants!'

Lil was jostled aside as the crowd rose to its feet, an emotional mob stirred into motion with only the gruesome spectacle of a hanging in mind. It seemed she'd arrived too late to save Jackson or warn the wagoners of the looming peril of an attack by a gang of marauders.

'Stop it!' she cried. 'Have you lost your heads? You're sick — misled!'

They were going to unchain Jackson from the wheel of Petrie's wagon, to drag him to some suitably limbed nearby tree and string him up. Misfit Lil's instincts were to rush after them, to fight them, to make use of her guns . . .

But she knew any of that would avail her nothing. While the wagoners were losing their heads, she had to use hers as never before.

And her frantic thoughts produced an imaginative course of action whereby she might still have a chance to pull off Jackson's and her escape, just.

She refined the desperate scheme as she ran back to Rebel, standing patiently and obediently on dropped reins. She unstrapped and delved into a saddlebag. In the bottom corners were her medicinal supplies. Many of them were based on old Indian cures; some of them she'd been taught about by Jackson himself. Nearly all were based on wild plants and the old-time skills of woodsmen, trailblazers and mountain men.

She found what she wanted in a small canvas bag. It looked like, and was, a tight bunch of broken, light-brown, tapering roots, long and round. Lil took a great wad of the stuff and packed it under her tongue, taking care to swallow none. The taste, even contained in one part of her mouth, was bitter and nauseous.

Then she ran after the crowd, who oblivious to everything except the task they had in hand, were leading Jackson to his execution. Though she was punched and pummelled, she forced her way through the mob to his very side.

He was startled and dismayed to see her.

'Go away, Lil!' he said urgently. 'You've come too late. There's nothing you can do for me now.' His grief swelled to match her own. 'Save yourself from this horror! For God's sake, run from death while you can!'

But Lil was working herself up to put on the most dramatic performance of her life.

'My love, I can't leave you like this! I must say a sad goodbye, and for future memory's sake seal it with a farewell kiss!'

The words came out thickly, because of the load under her tongue, but she hoped the listeners would discount the oddness in her voice as the result of emotion.

And they did.

When she flung her arms around Jackson's neck there were catcalls and jeers. They intensified as she placed her lips on his face.

'Feverwort in my mouth,' she mumbled in a whisper close to his ear. 'Open yours and kiss me!'

She could have easily said horse gentian, or tinker's weed, or the Indian purge. Any of these or several other names for the same plant product would have told the canny frontiersman what he needed to know and what he had to do.

Jackson Farraday had always refused to entertain the idea of a woman half his age as a sexual partner. Lil's love for him was an embarrassment — a huge problem, no less. She aspired to be a top scout, of worth to the military and others, exactly like himself. And she had the capability for it, which was an achievement he couldn't help himself admiring. But he was an honourable man who couldn't dally with a woman's affections unless he intended to marry her. With Lil, because of her age, he had long ago ruled matrimony out — but completely!

The common practice of marrying girls barely out of childhood was not for him. He couldn't bed for a wife a female who one day would still be in the May or June of life when he was in December.

But astonishingly — publicly, in full view of an avid audience that closely surrounded them — he now apparently broke all his rules to give Lil an open-mouthed kiss. Their lips slotted tightly together like they were trying to eat one another.

The emigrants were shocked, scandalized. In Godfearing, enlightened, white American society, such behaviour was immoral and outrageous.

'The trollop!'

'A harlot's kiss!'

'The hussy!'

'Pull them apart!'

Other lips pursed. Disgusted womenfolk, though not averse to witnessing a lynching, averted their eyes and turned their backs.

'Shameful!'

'Separate the pair! We don't need to see them going at their lusts!'

'It ain't decent!'

Lil was dragged off Jackson, leaving

the feverwort, unknown to his captors, in his mouth.

Surreptitiously, he masticated and swallowed the foul-tasting deposit Lil had pushed with her tongue into his mouth. Astringent and vile, the gooey, chewed gift burned his gullet. He had to fight hard not to gag or let his discomfort show as he swallowed hard and the acid-like bite trickled down to his stomach.

The wagoners shoved Jackson jubilantly toward the trunk of a thick-trunked, lone pine with sturdy, spreading limbs about eighteen feet above the ground. His own horse stood beneath the tree, saddled and with the stock of his long gun jutting from its scabbard as though mocking his tied and useless hands.

Some delay ensued while a strong rope was produced and argument was held about how to tie a hangman's knot.

'A hangman's noose must have thirteen coils.'

'No, six or eight is best.'

'Who cares? Break his neck or throttle him — makes no diff'rence!'

But the rope was finally thrown up and over a stout branch to dangle ominously, sinisterly four or so feet above the empty, waiting saddle.

Reiner egged the mob on. His eyes were feverishly bright. The final revenge was imminent.

'Boost him up, boys! Get that necktie on him!'

Winton Petrie and the Reverend James Hannigan were nowhere in sight. Lil presumed they'd washed their hands of the matter, relinquishing all responsibility for their followers' mad actions.

She felt a shiver down her spine and tears formed in her eyes, which she angrily brushed away with her sleeve.

'Jackson, come on!' she muttered a plea to herself. 'Oh, please let this work. You know what you have to do!'

Jackson did indeed, and he could hardly help it happening. His insides revolted. He couldn't have held down his rebelling stomach's contents if he'd wanted to.

He suddenly sagged and would have dropped to his knees if he wasn't being held up. He groaned and tried to put his hands to his belly. He retched violently.

Then up it all came in a liquid gurgle. A stream of smelly vomit spewed out of his mouth and splashed his self-appointed restrainers.

Jackson writhed in their hands as he threw up, making a steady, chest-heaving, breathtaking mess of himself.

It was Lil's cue.

She rushed back into the fray, screaming, grave grey eyes wide with alarm and horror.

'Oh, sweet Jesus! I know that smell. It's like when my poor sister died just recent! Started the self-same fashion. Folks, it's the cholera! You're doomed — you'll all die!'

Lil's 'sister' was a fiction, but the emigrants didn't know that.

The men holding Jackson dropped

him and backed off, brushing the flecks of vomit from their clothes and shaking their soiled hands.

The part of the mob nearest to them turned and fled in confusion, all yelling in fearful consternation. It was every man and woman for himself.

The cry of 'cholera' swept through the camp and arguments and fights broke out between those who'd handled Jackson and Lil and those who hadn't. No one wanted to be infected by their fellows whom they considered contaminated.

In the West, cholera epidemics struck extremely rapidly, affecting large numbers and causing many deaths. Even doctors could do next to nothing for the sufferers. A healthy pioneer in the morning could find himself quickly in the throes of abdominal cramps. By evening his highly contagious condition would have led to watery diarrhoea, dehydration and prostration.

Soon, an infected community would be burying him — maybe in a ditch or under a cutbank with dozens of like victims.

But Lil strode forward and jerked her hapless, abandoned hero to his feet. She pulled out a knife from its sheaf and cut his wrists free.

'Sorry, Jackson — we've got to ride out of here, fast!'

Jackson groaned. 'Don't worry, Lil — they won't touch us for a while. You did very, very well.'

'No! You don't know the half of it. A bunch of Reiner's old sidekicks is on its way to raid the wagon train — to ransack and kill!'

Jackson didn't question her information. From past experience, he knew he would be able trust her word and judgement implicitly in any crisis.

His legs weak, Lil helped him into his saddle. Defensively, she drew a gun before she went to fetch Rebel, but a weapon's threat wasn't needed since the wagon camp had descended into wholesale panic and was totally disinterested in opposing their flight.

Despite their trials being far from over, and the death of Honesty Petrie unresolved, Lil felt ridiculously pleased with herself. She'd proved in the face of potential disaster that she'd learned well her lessons in Indian medicine from Jackson and others.

The Iroquois tribe used feverwort to aid the healing of broken bones, giving it yet another name, boneset.

The Cherokee turned to it for colds and sore throats.

The Seminoles and Mohicans employed it to ease fevers.

The Meskwaki got rid of worms with it.

Other tribes had used the same plant to treat typhoid fever, pleurisy, head-aches, piles, pneumonia, rheumatism, period disorders and venereal disease. It was also taken as a laxative.

But universally among the Seminole Indians, the Koasati and Cherokee, feverwort was administered to cause vomiting . . . Indian purge. Studies by European medical men found it to be a powerful and reliable emetic.

Lil and Jackson struck out for Buzzard City, riding parallel to the crooked, dusty old roadway, using whatever cover they could without delaying their progress, which was largely in single file.

Jackson was sweating and his face was pale beneath its tan, but eventually, when they came abreast, he produced a weak smile.

'Indian lore beats lynch law!'

14

The Battle at the Wagon Camp

Lil was under no illusion that trouble had been averted for the Petrie wagon train, or that she and Jackson could regard their mistreatment as absolving them from any responsibility for its fate. Innocent women's and children's lives were at stake.

But what were they to do?

'What we need is the Army,' Lil said.

'Not a chance,' Jackson replied. 'We're miles from Fort Dennis. It'd take till tomorrow night to get troops here.'

'Probably longer if Lieutenant Mike Covington had anything to do with it,' Lil said critically.

Presently, Lil thought she spotted a faint banner of dust. She pulled at Rebel's reins; she halted. So did

Jackson. Both jumped down and pressed ears to the earth.

'About ten horses,' Jackson said. 'Agree?'

'It must be the McCanns!' Lil said. 'There'd not likely be another bunch of riders heading this way.'

Without a word, they got over leather again, bent to unship rifles, and backtracked. This time, as they rode they took even greater care to conceal their presence and the evidence of their passing.

'Luckily I know this country right well,' Jackson said. His eyes were bleak. 'We can't divert them — take them on ourselves — but we can fire our guns to give the wagoners due warning when the moment comes.'

Lil shuddered. To the outlaws from White's Hole, the wagon train symbolized wealth on wheels on which to feast their appetite for plunder. It was a kind of cannibalism — white man against white man. The thought was hateful and gave her goosebumps.

They elected to make their observation post in the cool green shadows of a clump of aspen that overlooked the wagon camp. Over their heads, between the tops of the trees, a bruise-blue evening sky was darkening.

Jackson said, 'I figure these raiders will scout out the camp's layout, then make their attack at full dark. Failing light will make it unlikely for the emigrants to see them until it's too late to prepare themselves.'

Lil nodded. 'Clyde McCann is a snaky cuss. He may even wait till the moon is up. The fool wagoners wouldn't let me tell them trouble was brewing. They won't see anything unusual. They won't know what's hit them!'

'But if we go down there now they'll start all over with the lynching nonsense. There's nothing we can do but wait.'

Contrary to popular belief, wagon trains were rarely circled defensively when they camped, but the heavily laden Petrie rigs were roughly in that configuration. It gave shelter from wind or unexpected night-time changes in weather. The emigrants' animals were corralled in the centre to prevent them running off or being preyed upon by the critters of the wild.

Though the McCann riders didn't show themselves, instinct — sixth sense — alerted both Jackson and Lil to the fact that they were in the vicinity.

'Where are you, you goddamn wolves?' Lil muttered as she gripped her rifle. 'Maybe we should fire the regular, three-shot warning of danger now, Jackson.'

Jackson shook his head.

'I don't think so. The McCanns might just carry on lying low, then the wagoners' bravest might send out a party in the direction of our shots and find only us. It'd prove a distraction that wouldn't better their position any. And you or I might get killed.'

'No, I guess you're right — it's a chance we can't take.'

An hour passed, and another; waiting, like statues with tiring, straining eyes. When the moon rose, it was easy to see why the Conestogas, with their canvas tops, waterproofed with linseed oil and stretched over frameworks of hoop-shaped slats, were called prairie schooners. They gleamed whitely in a calm silver sea of light: sailing ships of the land.

Then the outlaws stealthily showed themselves, riding in on muffled hoofs from the dusky shadows in the direction of the creek. And all hell broke loose.

Jackson jerked off the three shots at the precise moment Lil told him, 'Something moving down there!'

The raiders recovered promptly from the surprise that their presence was somehow betrayed. Several of them whirled their mounts in the direction of the aspen grove, jammed in spurs and raced upslope, unleashing a torrent of blazing gunfire.

Fortunately, the outlaws had no clear

targets. From the trees' shadows, Lil and Jackson, moving fast and constantly, gave as good as they got. Legs freed from the long tension of waiting, carried them from one vantage point to another in swift succession, creating an effect that the outlaws' raid had been discovered by a posse of law enforcers or bounty men.

Lil allowed one tall, dreadlocked fellow to come into deadly range. She sighted on him and squeezed off a shot.

The ruffian dropped his reins, clasped his holed chest and pitched from his saddle. His loose horse, turned away, dragging him, broken left foot caught up in a stirrup.

The horse crashed into the mount of one its riders' companions. Horses and men were reduced to a thrashing tangle of dust-raising legs and bodies. Squeals and screams rang out hideously.

'C'mon, you scum!' Lil yelled. 'C'mon and get yours!'

Levering and firing rapidly, Lil quickly emptied her rifle's magazine.

Since she had another box of .44 centre-fire cartridges in a saddlebag, she retreated, ducking and weaving, to where she and Jackson had left their horses in safety, far back under the trees. She was confronted by an unexpected sight.

Deke McCann, on foot and limping, was trying to mount Rebel, who repeatedly sidestepped as his foot touched the left stirrup.

'Stand still, you ornery bangtail!'

Unhorsed, he was evidently planning to desert his comrades and quit the fight before it properly began.

'Hold it, hoss thief!' Lil rapped.

Deke swung. His jaw dropped in disbelief.

'You, by God! But we left you with the whore . . .'

Though the bully seemingly had a yellow streak, he reached for the Colt revolver at his hip. It was obvious he wasn't aware of Lil's skill and speed with a handgun.

'Yeah,' Lil said, 'Broken-Nose Ginny

would've sent her love, but she don't like *rats*!'

Fast as Deke's hand dropped, Lil was faster.

Lil's bullets took him full in the upper body, hammering out the percussion of death. They cleaved through cloth, flesh and muscle; broke bone. One lodged in his heart. Another emerged between his shoulderblades. As he thumped face-first into the leaf mould carpeting the hard ground, Lil saw a gaping exit hole, jetting blood; the hanging bits of internal flesh blasted out of him and hanging in pulpy pink strings from the edge of the wound.

She had no sorrow. He had been a worthlesss human being and she felt nothing for him. For sure, he would have had no compunction about killing her.

Meanwhile, the wagoners, alerted by the commotion, had swung into defensive action under the command of Winton Petrie in longjohns and nightshirt. He moved around a hastily mustered circle of shooters, taking huge risks with his own safety, to organize the operation against the yelling marauders who had swooped on them out of the darkness. His white face was mottled with anger.

Withering fire was soon pouring from the wagons and the bulk of the McCann bunch found itself caught between what seemed like two forces. Nonetheless, a devastating battle developed in the moonlight. Red flashes of gunfire and clouds of gunsmoke tore up the night's silver peace.

The outlaws — there were some ten of them — had counted on the factor of surprise, since they were outnumbered by their proposed victims. When the tables had been turned by the noisy interruption Jackson and Lil staged from behind them, it changed the odds. A hail of fire was ready to meet them by the time they could storm the wagons in earnest.

They received the worst of the clash. Another outlaw's horse went down. A one-time king of Utah rustlers, lured into the expedition by the promise of easy booty, cussed obscenely as the stock of his rifle was smashed into splinters.

A big, bearded, bloodstained White's Hole hardcase roared in dismay, 'You lied to us, Clyde McCann! You brung us into the jaws of a trap!'

At close quarters, he raised a six-gun and shot the outlaw leader in the head.

He swung his horse's head away from the wagon camp and led a disorderly but complete flight of what was left of his victim's scratch gang.

Incredibly, the action had lasted less than seven minutes. The rattle of gunfire from the wagons came to a stop with the attack routed and five surviving outlaws in hasty retreat. For a few moments, jubilation took hold among the wagoners.

But it quickly turned to wails of grief.

The raid had been no kinder to the emigrants. They, too, had their dead — six men and one woman — and those snatched cruelly from them included the wagonmaster, Winton Petrie, drilled though the heart.

'This is a nightmare,' said a woman who'd been abruptly widowed. 'What will I do now?'

Jackson and Lil, who'd ridden down into the shaken camp and flung off their horses to give what first-aid they could to the shattered party, had no easy answer for the poor, husbandless woman.

'But maybe death was a merciful release for Mister Petrie,' Lil said quietly to Jackson. 'He truly wasn't himself after Honesty was found murdered.'

Among the badly wounded was Luke Reiner, or Mark Steiner. Lil and Jackson found him coughing blood, surrounded by a small, shocked crowd. It was plain he was dying; his wounds were not survivable, although there was little external bleeding. He had two holes in him — in the upper midriff — and was in considerable pain. But he was determined to do mischief to the end.

Jackson urged him to clear his conscience of the lies he had told about his, Jackson's, alleged relations with Honesty.

'Come clean, Reiner — or Steiner,' he said. 'I know all about your past. The McCanns told Lil Goodnight what your game was. Why not explain the rest — here, before you face a day of higher judgement?'

Reiner only grunted, baulking at the suggestion.

'It must of been you, Farraday! Sure weren't me that killed the kid. Why would I a-done that?'

Lil broke in impulsively.

'See here, Reiner, the McCanns exploded your windies. You were never in the saloon or anywhere else in Buzzard City when you said you were. You were out someplace collecting the proceeds of an old robbery, which we'll surely find in your saddle packs.'

Reiner got crafty. 'Don't prove I

killed Honesty Petrie, do it? And the McCanns are dead. You can't support no testimony. You got nothin' on me thataway!'

'You tried to murder me, too. You drygulched me on the road to Buzzard City.'

Reiner scorned the charge. 'Mebbe, but you're still alive, ain't you?'

More blood trickled from his lips and he summoned the last of his vehemence.

'Naw, folks, lissen here! It were this bitch's fine amigo Farraday as killed dear, two-timin' Honesty. The dirty ol' man shouldn't get away with it. String 'im up! Don't let this range slut cheat the hangrope o' his rotten neck. Seize the pair o' them!'

The wagoners did listen and were divided, though in the new, dire circumstances no one in the outlaw-savaged company had the inclination to form another lynch mob.

A burly blacksmith said, 'Why should a dying man lie to us? Mebbe he didn't go to Buzzard City, maybe he did drygulch Misfit Lil, but it sure don't prove the balance of the case — that it was him killed Honesty Petrie.'

The newly widowed woman began crying again.

'There's been too much killing already. We only wanted to start afresh in Californy. Why can't we go on from this terrible, godforsaken place — wipe the slate clean?'

The blacksmith said, 'An innocent girl was ravished and put to death. There must be civilized justice brought to a lawless land. We can't just close this thing like a book, as if it were a crime never done.'

Surprisingly to the doubters of his innocence in the matter, Jackson said, 'Amen to that!'

Then Reiner gave a sudden ghastly, rattling cry. 'Aaaargh . . . ' After which he gasped with his last breath, '*It weren't me!*' and died.

It wasn't him . . .

Somehow, despite the messages her

heart was trying to trumpet, Lil believed Reiner. Her sensible head argued that Reiner had known he was on death's doorstep and making trouble for Jackson Farraday and herself was not sufficient reason for him to continue lying about the murder.

He wasn't Honesty's killer. Nor, of course, was Jackson.

But if Reiner wasn't, who was? And why?

The breakthrough wasn't so very long in coming.

15

'You Know, Then?'

Women and children had broken into a flood of weeping. Not all the men were dry-eyed. In no time at all the absence of the Reverend James Hannigan, his wife, daughter and wagon came to notice.

The reverend's services, and the comfort of faith in a hereafter, were required by his flock in the presence of death. But it was discovered that in the aftermath of the tumultuous gun battle and the surprising return of Jackson Farraday and Misfit Lil — fugitives who'd turned saviours — Hannigan's rig had slipped quietly away.

And it dawned on Lil that she was the one in the best position to know why. The shock of it made her feel weak-kneed. All at once, in the blinding flash she'd always thought was the creation of someone's vivid imagination, she knew who had killed Honesty Petrie, and how.

'Lil, you've gone awful pale,' Jackson said. 'Do you want to sit down?'

'No, I never realized . . . didn't think it through when I should have . . . put it all together . . . '

Jackson was regarding her solicitously. She supposed she must sound stupid, lost, and pulled her shattered wits together.

'If it's what I think, I need to ride out and find the Reverend Hannigan and Prudence!'

'Then you must let me come with you,' Jackson said. He didn't think to question her decision. The decamping of the Hannigans was plainly of vital importance to his young friend. He knew her well enough to know that she wouldn't be pursuing some hysterical whim. Misfit Lil wasn't like that.

Weary and dirty though they were, they climbed back into their saddles and loped over to the roadway.

'North-east,' Lil said, pointing them in that direction. 'They wouldn't have gone the other way. That would be the trail taken by the last of the outlaws, toward White's Hole.'

It was still hours before dawn. The air was cold and a lack of wind lent a dreamy silence to the rugged, shadowed landscape whenever they halted their horses to check for the Hannigans' fresh tracks. Though their eyes were eager as well as weary, they wasted no energy on talk, apart from consulting on sign. The first objective was to find the absconding Hannigans.

The road was an ascending one, leading to a high ridge. It would make the going slow for the Hannigans' laden wagon. They caught up with it inside an hour on a stretch with an abyss of blackness to the left and a long, rocky slope to the right. In daylight, they knew the view on the left to be a dizzying one into a deep gorge through which coursed the same waters in which Honesty's body had been found.

'Pull up, Hannigan!' Jackson shouted. 'You can't outrun us. An explanation is called for and we mean to have it.'

Hannigan reined up his team and set the brake.

'What do you want with us?' he blustered. 'By what right do you accost us?'

Mabel Hannigan, the drab wife with the faded eyes, appeared from within the wagon.

'We've done no wrong!' she said waspishly. 'You can't delay us! Winton Petrie is dead and his expedition is terminated.'

Hannigan shushed her.

Prudence appeared behind her mother. She looked shy. Or was it sly? Or maybe frightened.

She had a tight, haunted look about her eyes and heavy lips.

'Lil! I didn't expect to see you again,' she said in a small voice for such a large girl. 'It's no good. You can't do anything to help. No one can. Papa has decided it's best for us to go.'

She sounded oddly resigned. It was difficult for Lil to see in her the same robust girl who'd dared to explore, in a stolid way, beyond the boundaries of her restricted life with her bubbly young companion, Honesty Petrie.

'It's no good, Prudence,' Lil said. 'It's time for the truth to come out and for you to admit the lie that's told by your name. Prudent you haven't been — maybe never have!'

'You know, then?'

Lil nodded. 'I'm sure I do. Just as your pa and ma do. And the three of you can't be allowed to run away from it, leaving Mister Farraday under suspicion, his name blackened, his very life threatened by a miscarriage of justice.'

Hannigan barked, 'My daughter was of unsound mind! She was led astray by the forces of the Devil! How do you know what really happened? How will anyone?'

'Because I shall tell them under oath

what I heard with my own ears and saw with my own eyes.'

'You weren't there!' Hannigan countered. 'What could you have seen?'

Jackson said heavily, fingering his saddle gun butt, 'I think we'd better all set down and discuss this.'

'I don't think so.'

Jackson sighed. 'Get down, preacherman! Your wife and daughter, too. Get down and stand easy. All we want is for you to tell the truth. Is that much to ask of a God-loving holy man and his family?'

'And we mean to have the truth!' Lil added tersely. 'Climb down off that seat, or Mister Farraday'll come up there and make you!'

The preacher continued briefly to stare at the Westerner pair, thought better of what further objection was forming on his lips, and began coming down.

'Very well,' he said, less than temperately. 'What purpose this will serve, I don't know.'

But he left his high perch and his high-and-mighty tone. His wife and daughter followed him meekly. Lil and Jackson dismounted. They all stood face to face. Some eyes met; others avoided the contact.

Lil said, 'Look, Reverend, there can't be any question of Prudence's guilt. I'll force the confession from her myself if I have to.'

'Ah! Then you admit you weren't there?'

'I was there a time before, when Prudence and Honesty pleasured themselves in a similar fashion. They were together at a river's edge under the pretext of bathing. At first, they thought they were alone and that I didn't know what they were up to.'

At that juncture, Prudence started to cry.

'She was so lovely,' she blubbered. 'I didn't mean to do it. It was an accident. I should have stopped myself, but it was the most lovely thing in my life, and I couldn't.'

'Silence, child!' Hannigan roared.

But the irony was Prudence was in another situation where she was unable to stop herself once she'd started. Insensible to her father's command, she stumbled on.

'I straddled her, like we usually did . . . her face was under me and I — I became reckless. We'd done it often. But this time, when I recovered from my — my fit, she — she . . . '

Everyone stared at her, absorbed, shocked.

Prudence could scarcely carry on, but the concluding words came in a sudden rush. 'I found she was suffocated!'

Hannigan put his hands over his ears and hung his head, overwhelmed by the shame and embarrassment brought upon him.

'I'm ruined! Ruined!'

The drab mother screeched, 'Hush your mouth, you idiot child! It's unnatural. They'll lock you up in the insane asylum for life!'

'It's an abomination in the eyes of the Lord!' Hannigan moaned.

Lil wondered if the self-aggrandizing sky-pilot had room for any sympathy for the dead girl, or his daughter. Obviously, he had none for Jackson Farraday, whom he'd left to face the fury whipped up by Luke Reiner's genuinely ignorant accusations.

The tears and words continued to tumble from Prudence.

In her mind's eye, Lil reconstructed the awful scene. Indulging in more silliness by moonlight on the secluded creek bank, the heavily built Prudence had accidentally snuffed the vivacious life out of her slightly built partner. Secret gratification, spiced by guilt, would have been suddenly supplanted by overwhelming grief, then fear and panic.

'I didn't want to die for what I'd done to Honesty in my giddy insensibility,' Prudence sobbed. 'When I knew she was dead, I was terrified — there by myself with her pretty little body. So I kissed her and said I would love her always, and pushed her out into the creek, so it would look like she'd drowned. And I prayed to God for forgiveness for my sin.'

'A blasphemy!' Hannigan cried. 'The girl's confession must be suppressed. She doesn't know what she's saying. She must be committed — '

Lil said, 'Be quiet, you sanctimonious old fool! She was thoughtless, but she wasn't consciously evil.'

Hannigan shut up but didn't respond to her disdain.

'No! No!' Prudence wept. 'Honesty's blood is on my hands as surely as if I cut her throat! Nothing will ever be the same again. I don't want to live — I want to die — to go to my sweet Honesty!'

'Look out!' Jackson shouted. 'Hold her, someone!'

Prudence, despite her bulk, moved with astonishing swiftness, like a deer surprised in the forest. She ran from the small gathering beside the wagon to the roadway's edge at the left.

And when she reached the edge, she kept on going, right out into nothingness as though she would walk on the air, her legs threshing.

Then she fell into the darkness, out of sight.

She didn't cry out. She made no vocal sounds. But they heard the rustling crashes as her heavy body hit the treetops far below, close to the probable bottom of the canyon. Just possibly, the crashes ended with a soft but chilling thud that had no echo, though Lil decided afterwards that she may have only imagined that.

'Oh, Lord,' Mabel Hannigan said in a quavering voice. 'We did the best we could.'

Lil said to Jackson alone, and through her teeth, 'I'd hate to see their worst.'

It was a long and cold wait for first light. When it finally came, Lil and Jackson fixed ropes and went down to retrieve Prudence's big but broken body.

She was dead, of course, her neck and many other bones broken so her limbs were at grotesque angles. A depression was in her skull, deforming her expression enigmatically.

Jackson placed a kerchief over her face and looked up into Lil's sad eyes as he knelt down by the twisted and battered figure.

'Save your tears,' he told her. 'We'll be safe now, and I think so will she, in a strange way.'

Lil studied on that for a moment.

'Yes, she will, away from her dreadful parents. Who knows? Maybe she really is back with her dainty but naughty little Honesty.'

*   *   *

The Reverend James and Mabel Hannigan were escorted back to the wagon train camp. The preacher's wife spent the while in prayer, beseeching help and comfort in their deep tribulations. After a conference, it was decided the party

— now leaderless and many mourning dead loved ones — should return to Silver Vein under the guidance of Jackson Farraday and Lil Goodnight.

There, a full report was filed on the Petrie party's various misfortunes, but the lackadaisical sheriff, Hamish Howard, was disinclined to pursue the matter, seeing in it no personal profit and a deal of awkward work. The Petrie expedition was officially broken up. Some families went north to Fort Bridger, to join other emigrants and continue the trek west by more orthodox routes. Others decided they'd had enough and returned to their old hometowns in the East or settled in Utah.

Within days, the Army called for the benefit of Jackson Farraday's services as a civilian scout in another territory. Misfit Lil made sure she was on hand to say goodbye when he hit the trail before sunrise. She was the only one around so early.

'Thank you again for your help over the wagon train disaster, Lil,' Jackson said. 'Most of all for saving my neck from a lynch mob's noose.'

'Think nothing of it. It was purely a pleasure,' she said with an impish smile. 'You might say I freed you with a kiss. For a reward, won't you let me have another? Just once!'

Since no one was about, he reached across the narrow space between their horses and placed one hand over hers. She leaned close from her saddle.

He kissed her full on the lips.

When he rode on, Lil's heart was still thumping and a song was left in her blood.

THE END

We do hope that you have enjoyed reading this large print book.

Did you know that all of our titles are available for purchase?

We publish a wide range of high quality large print books including:
Romances, Mysteries, Classics
General Fiction
Non Fiction and Westerns

Special interest titles available in large print are:
The Little Oxford Dictionary
Music Book, Song Book
Hymn Book, Service Book

Also available from us courtesy of Oxford University Press:
Young Readers' Dictionary
(large print edition)
Young Readers' Thesaurus
(large print edition)

For further information or a free brochure, please contact us at:
Ulverscroft Large Print Books Ltd.,
The Green, Bradgate Road, Anstey,
Leicester, LE7 7FU, England.
Tel: (00 44) 0116 236 4325
Fax: (00 44) 0116 234 0205

THE TOMBSTONE VENDETTA

Ralph Hayes

When Billy Clanton and his friends are murdered in Tombstone by the town marshal and his deputies, the growing tension between the local authorities and the ranchers spirals out of control. The once sleepy frontier town is mired in hatred, with bad blood and scores to settle on both sides. Families are torn asunder as the violence rages on. Will there ever be peace in Tombstone? Or will peace only come when one side reigns victorious?

LAND OF THE LOST

Dean Edwards

Young drifter Hal Harper's welcome to the town of Senora is to look down the barrels of the law — little knowing that the outlaw Tate Talbot and his gang are the elected sheriff and deputies. Talbot, with a wanted poster on his head worth a fortune, decides to collect his own bounty by killing the innocent Harper and claiming the drifter is the outlaw known as Diamond Bob Casey. Harper escapes — but only into the Land of the Lost . . .